CW00684381

DOG
MOVES
IN A
MYSTERIOUS
WAY

Copyright © 2023 by Rob Badcock
Published by Fenrir Fonts

Cover design by Spiffing Covers Ltd

All rights reserved

Paperback ISBN: 978-1-7384162-1-9
eBook ISBN: 978-1-7384162-0-2

No part of this book may be reproduced in any form or by any
electronic or mechanical means including information storage
and retrieval systems, without permission in writing from the
author. The only exception is by a reviewer, who may quote
short excerpts in a review.

This book is a work of fiction. Names, characters, places, and
incidents either are products of the author's imagination or are
used fictitiously. Any resemblance to actual persons, living or
dead, events, or locales is entirely coincidental.

DOG

MOVES
IN A
MYSTERIOUS
WAY

ROB BADCOCK

Also by Rob Badcock

Big Frog
The Fearance
Third Stone
Quarantine Cave

CONTENTS

ASH THURSDAY

The man in seat 17A blinked his eyes open. He was most surprised to find himself on an aeroplane. He was even more surprised to see a chicken sitting beside him. A quick glance across the aisle told him that he hadn't woken up on a chicken flight. To his relief, all the other occupants were humans, like him. He appeared to be the only traveller with a chicken as a companion. On the seat next to the chicken lay a book, open at page 57.

A fierce-looking woman in seat 17D was clearly unhappy with the situation and reached up to press the call button.

'Yes, madam?' said the young stewardess with a warm, friendly smile. It was her first flight.

'That man has a chicken sitting next to him!'

Young Tiffany stared at the bird, stared at that man, then stared back at the bird, mouth agape. The chicken, unwilling to be drawn into a staring contest, concentrated on the emergency procedures notice stuffed into the seat pocket in front of it. *If I can't see you, you can't see me…*

Still wearing a fixed smile, the stewardess backed down the aisle all the way to the galley, where she reported the incident to her superior, a battle-scarred trolley warrior named Brenda.

'A chicken? You're pulling my leg, girl.'

'No, it definitely was a chicken.'

'A chicken? How the fuck did that get on board?'

'I don't know. I...'

Without waiting for an answer, Brenda pushed her way past the girl and barrelled down the aisle. It wasn't as if she wasn't totally unprepared to find an item of live poultry sitting on her plane, but when she did, she exploded. A fucking chicken! On her watch!

The man followed the chicken's lead by staring out of the window. The bird had nothing to do with him. Besides, a chicken sitting beside him was the least of his problems. There followed much flapping of wing and much swearing of stewardess before the chicken finally went peacefully, but not before leaving a runny, yellow splat of a calling card, just to make sure no one took its seat.

The plane banked sharply to present breathtaking views of a snow-capped mountain range. White ridges intersected by black chasms stretched as far as the eye could see. Where the hell was he? The hum of the window against his cheek made him feel drowsy. *He felt as if he had been travelling forever.* Within a matter of seconds, the man in seat 17A was asleep.

'Excuse me, sir.' It took a third shake of the shoulder to pull him from the deep. He sat bolt upright with a jerk and stared wide-eyed at the young Tiffany. 'We've landed, sir. Time to disembark.'

He struggled to a half stand, slid out of his seat and followed her to the exit, where she stood to attention.

'Goodbye, sir, and thank you for flying Monarch Airlines.'

He took a deep breath and headed out into the bright sunlight. The heat hit him like a hammer. Halfway down the steps, he was halted by a cry.

'Sir, you forgot your book!' The wannabe fly me skipped

down the steps to hand him the paperback. The book wasn't his. The chicken wasn't his. But here was not the time or place to argue, so he took it.

He felt his lips move. He heard himself say, in a voice he hardly recognised, 'Where are we?'

'Napoli, sir. Naples. See Naples and die!' she laughed.

***

The ice clinked against the sides of the chunky, cut-glass tumbler as he raised the whisky to his lips. The warmth of the malt on his palate was real, the only thing akin to any kind of reality since he'd woken on the plane. What he had in his mouth was distilled, peaty and expensive. That much he knew.

Behind him on the bed lay a passport open at a name and face he didn't know. Colin Barker, it read. It wasn't him. Problem was, right now, he couldn't come up with a better suggestion. He closed his eyes and let the liquor slip down his throat.

On the plus side, he hadn't seen Naples and died. In fact, all that he'd seen of the place was through a grimy coach window, as the driver edged his way through a seething sea of traffic married with a constant cacophony of car horns. There'd been men standing in groups on street corners and barefoot boys kicking a ball about in a dark alleyway. It looked rough.

They finally broke clear of the city to follow a main highway passing through low-rise settlements, all painted white. To the right, there was a wide bay, to the left, a volcano.

A volcano… Why didn't that surprise him? At least, there hadn't been a chicken sitting next to him.

The travel rep, who had appeared from nowhere to grab

him at the airport, now stood up at the front of the coach.

'In half an hour, we shall be arriving in Sorrento. The temperature is a beautiful thirty degrees, and you will have this for the whole of your week's stay, with no forecast of rain.' A little cheer went up. 'Our first stop will be at the Imperial Hotel Tramontano,' she said, fixing a pointed stare in his direction. That must be him, then.

Front desk had welcomed him warmly. 'You are in room 48, sir. We think you will like it. Best view in the hotel, sir. Your room is ready and the porter has taken your case up.'

Case? What case?

'Your stay is fully paid for, sir. Just charge any extras to your room.'

Paid for?

'We have booked a table for you in the restaurant at seven, sir. We hope you enjoy your stay.'

So the extras began with a brace of whiskies in the bar, followed by a carry-out, for good measure. And they had certainly been right about the room: high ceiling, polished parquet floor, floral wallpaper, marble-topped desk and large French windows opening out onto a balcony with one of the most breathtaking views he'd ever seen. The Bay of Naples, shimmering in the haze of the hot sun, was being criss-crossed by small passenger boats, presumably ferrying trippers out to the small islands he could make out to his left. The sea was a deep blue, as deep a blue as he'd ever seen. Apart from… apart from…

He glanced over at the king-size bed, with its plump white duvet and large fluffy pillows. It was calling his name, whatever that was. With a degree of difficulty, he levered himself out of the soft leather armchair and shuffled over to the bed, a tad unsteady on his feet. The passport he placed with exaggerated care on the bedside table and picked up the book the stewardess had thrust into his hand.

It was a dog-eared paperback which had clearly passed through a number of hands. Dusty, too, a thin, red film suggesting it might have once belonged to a gold prospector or fossil hunter. He'd clearly had too much to drink. He smiled, as he looked round for the waste bin, before recalling it was in the bathroom under the sink. For a moment, he considered making the trek across the parquet expanse, then thought better of it and flopped onto the bed, book still in hand.

He lay on his back and closed his eyes. So tired, so tired. Yet the weird, unexplainable happenings of the day would not let him go. Who had bought him a ticket for a trip to Italy, all expenses paid? More importantly, how come he couldn't remember anything before the moment he woke up on the plane? Was his name *really* Colin Barker? What the fuck was happening to him? With every unanswered question, he could feel himself becoming more agitated, so he picked up the book. It fell open in his hands on page 57…

I look forward to the training sessions; beats the monotony of cage and compound. So here I am, waiting patiently, standing like a good boy, waiting for the command. Looks like we're ready to go…

Yakka, yakka, yakka! DZIT!

Okay, okay, I get the message. You really don't have to shout. Now how about the praise and reward? I snatch at the dried biscuit and gulp it down. Interesting, Aggie seems to be on good form today. That was a 30-second down. Usually bottom of the class and naughty with it. Pissed in the middle of the big yellow bendy tunnel last week and wouldn't come out. Boy, did she pay for that.

Mmm… hold on a minute. My nose tells me her handler is giving her a different treat. I edge closer. I'm getting bacon, I'm getting tuna and, oh my god, could it be… liver? No wonder she's jumping through hoops!

Yakka, yakka, yakka. WRALKIES!

So we are all led up and down on our leads. Right turn. Left turn. About turn. Yakka, yakka, yakka. SHTAND! We all stand, waiting for the pat and the treat. We walk on. A late arrival appears, offering a smile of apology in the hope it will wash with Handler. It never ceases to amaze me how so-called intelligent beings will insist on dragging us behind them when we are trying to squat for a crap, as is the case here. It's Harry!

Harry's the most popular guy in the class; he's the life and soul of the party who is always up to tricks. Right now, his trick is to try to hop and shit at the same time. Of course, this sets us all off, screaming with laughter. You can stick your right turn, left turn up your arse, 'cos we're all going to jump up and down and shout at our mate. Harry! Harry!

But something's up! Normally, Harry would shout back at us and try to yank his handler's arm out of its socket. Not this time. He creeps along on his belly, like a scared cat, tears in his eyes.

'What's up, mate?' I ask, when he reaches us.

'They've chopped me balls off,' he mutters.

'What!' A quick glance confirms this to be the horrific truth. Where a fine pair of clackers once proudly hung, there's nothing. Harry was the life and soul of the party no more. Our conversation is cut short by a jerk on my lead. Yakka. Yakka. DJOWN!

'Yes, Miss! Whatever you say, Miss!'

The curtain drapes rustled in the warm breeze drifting through the window, the hazy engine sound of ferries fading into the distance. Still on his back, he drifted into a deep slumber and let the book drop onto the floor.

***

The man in room 48 blinked his eyes open. Half expecting to be waking on a plane, he sat bolt upright and looked around the room. Imperial Hotel Tramontano. A cake of dried whisky had formed in the corners of his mouth. Front desk words nudged him further into the land of the living. *We have booked you a table in the restaurant at seven, sir.* What time was it now? Had he overslept?

He looked at his watch. Except that it couldn't possibly be his watch. The big hand of the gold Rolex pointed to the eight. The small hand of the gold Rolex pointed to between the six and the seven. Torn between two panics – being late for dinner and how to explain the Rolex on his wrist – he chose to focus on the dinner option.

One quick, cold shower later, he was standing staring at the contents of the wardrobe. He chose a pair of cream chinos, a blue-and-white-striped shirt of crisp cotton, both perfectly ironed, and a pair of soft leather yacht shoes. Yacht shoes? Why not? A quick check of the Rolex told him it was five to.

Thankfully, the restaurant was easy to find, just two flights of broad, red-carpeted stairs up to a landing adorned with very old-looking oil paintings. A couple were waiting at the podium. Him: dark blue blazer, white shirt, grey leather loafers, denim jeans – with a crease – hair too big for his age, crimped like a plate of crinkle-cut chips. Had to be English.

Her: green wallpaper dress, pink shoes. Tights. Had to be English.

'Do you think we'll get in, darling? It looks fully booked,' she said.

'Look and learn, darling,' he smiled.

With the look of a suspicious bloodhound, the elderly head waiter approached, face all a grimace.

Before he had time to speak, Grey Shoes stepped forward to offer a handshake. 'I'm afraid we do not have a reservation, but...' In one smooth movement, old jowly chops folded both hands around the man's as if greeting a long-lost friend. The crumpled note was discreetly transferred, the transaction completed and the couple ushered through to a window table.

A quick scan of the restaurant revealed there to be only one table left, a small, circular two-seater. Right beside the door marked *Toilette*. Ah, so this was the price he had to pay for the all-inclusive, free stay – pizza by the pisser. Or maybe, just maybe, he could try that bribe-the-waiter stunt pulled by Grey Shoes. A quick search of his pockets drew a blank. No cash. *Just charge expenses to your room...*

'Ah, Signor Barker!'

Before he could recoil, Bloodhound had an arm round his shoulders and was leading him into the dining room. The hubbub of conversation dropped as all eyes turned to watch the unlikely couple thread their way through the tables and out through a door on the far side. With a bow, the waiter showed him out onto a terrace where there was laid a table for one. Crisp, white linen cloth, silver cutlery, elegant wine glasses with oranges and lemons motif. And before him, as if for his eyes only, spread the Bay of Naples, the smog-thickened haze hanging above the city on the far shore clearing along the curve of the coastline to reveal the volcano, standing watch, standing guard. The dishes came and came and came, starting off innocently with breads, fat olives and dipping oils. Of course, he'd taken far too much. The hams next, sliced so thin you could almost see through them, followed by a broth so delicate you could weep. He had never tasted food like it. A crisp white wine from somewhere called Abruzzo paved the way for a velvet earthy red. The waitress, Maria, recommended a 1972 Barolo for the main course. She spoke in a mixture of Italian and English, just enough for him to understand, just enough to leave a sensual hint of the unknown.

It had all gone perfectly until the *secondi* arrived. Maria proudly presented a silver serving dish with a dome, which she removed with a flourish and stepped back.

'*Scaloppine di pollo al limone!* Chicken with...'

'No!' he heard himself scream.

In an instant, Bloodhound appeared from nowhere. 'Signor Barker! Is anything wrong?' The girl withdrew, tears in her eyes.

'No, please... I'm sorry. But I... can't eat... chicken...'

A chargrilled *bistecca* was soon produced, smiles were shared, apologies accepted, bridges mended. In halting, sultry tones, Maria told him she'd visited London.

'Buckingham Palace, Madame Tussauds, Hard Rock Cafe. It is very beautiful.'

'Yes, it is. Very beautiful.'

'And you, Signor, do you live in London?'

'Me? London? Er, yes.' Of course I do...

After the final plate had been cleared he sat, warmed cognac glass in the cup of his hand, soaking in the stunning vista spread before him. Dusk fell second by second, pinpricks of light growing in confidence until the whole coastline was a-twinkle. The autostrada the coach had taken from Naples stood out like a string of fairy lights. When was that? Was that only today? Having added a hefty tip to the already eye-watering bill, he tottered back to room 48, where he climbed into bed without brushing his teeth. No sooner did his head hit the pillow, than he heard a sound from the vestibule. Someone had slipped an envelope under his door.

***

Next morning, with a head like a bag of chisels, he levered himself out of bed, took a never-ending pee, splashed his face with cold water then stood and stared at the envelope patiently waiting outside the bathroom door. It was from the Citalia rep.

Welcome Meeting. Grand Salon. 10.00.

Inside was a leaflet of trips, tickets and timetables. The ridiculous Rolex – so heavy on his wrist he could hardly lift it – told him it was 9.30. It was make-your-mind-up time, the last thing he needed.

Breakfast? Out of the question. No way he could guarantee keeping anything down. Back to bed? No bad idea. Could he really be bothered to get dressed, just for a meeting? The Italian silk socks on his feet, the cream chinos on his legs and the blue-striped shirt on his body told him that he didn't have to worry about getting dressed. He'd gone to bed with his clothes on. Decision made.

The Grand Salon proved easy to find, directly across the

tiled foyer from reception. Two minutes to ten and the two front rows were almost full. He took a seat on the end of the back row. Scanning the expectant party before him, he vaguely recognised a few people from the coach ride. There was a couple in their thirties with two young boys. Another pair kitted out as if about to attempt an assault on Kilimanjaro, all beanie hat and backpack.

'Welcome to the Imperial Hotel Tramontano,' beamed the rep. 'You have chosen probably the best hotel in beautiful Sorrento for your stay, with its classic style and stunning gard...'

'Excuse me! Is this the welcome meeting?'

All heads turned to stare at the late arrivals. All except the man from room 48. He didn't need to. He recognised the voice as belonging to Grey Shoes, no doubt with Floral Wallpaper in tow.

'What do you think it is, a fucking chimpanzees' tea party?' he muttered under his breath, as did the rep. He had no desire to be in the same room as the couple, besides which he needed some fresh air. Such was the commotion caused by them insisting on taking the two vacant seats bang slap in the middle of the second row, that he was able to slip out unnoticed.

Once outside, he was hit with a wave of heavy scent from the brightly coloured climbers cascading down from the ornate metal frames flanking the main drive. Gravel walkways meandered through groves of mature trees, bark peeling to reveal sun-bleached trunks. Hidden away behind the lush planting, he found a tempting kidney-shaped swimming pool and promised himself a visit later. Already, he could feel the burn of a strengthening sun on the back of his neck so decided to head back to his room.

Taking the ancient lift was a mistake. It shuddered to a sickening standstill at every single floor, even though no one was there when the doors parted. On entering his room, he was surprised to find that it had already been serviced – bed made, clean towels, curtains pinned back. That was weird. How long had he been gone for? Half an hour? His head hurt too much to think harder, so he made straight for the open balcony to draw in lungfuls of air through his nose. For a full minute he stood there, eyes closed, his hands gripping the rail, just soaking in the sounds of the bay.

When he finally opened his eyes, he looked down to see that the hotel was perched right on the edge of a sheer cliff, a dizzying drop of some fifty metres to the sea below. Directly beneath his balcony was a series of pontoons and bathing huts forming a small lido. A solitary woman was swimming backstroke, looking up at him…

Turning back into the room, he noticed the dog book on the bed. Hadn't he thrown that in the bin? Of more interest was the wallet beside it. Light tan leather, soft to the touch. A quick flick open showed nothing inside. No cards, photos, receipts, but… it didn't feel empty. The answer lay in the middle section. Bank notes, crisp and new. Few in number, but each packing a punch – 500 euros, ten in all. His hand was shaking. He needed a drink. Hair of the dog.

'There you are, Signor. *Nastro Azzurro.*'

'Thank you,' he said, mouth full of pretzel. Having spent a miniscule slice of his new-found wealth on a straw hat from the gift shop, he'd found his way to the main square, *Piazza Tasso*, where he'd taken an outside table at a place called *Cafe Fauno*. Served in a tall, elegant glass, the ice-cold beer was swiftly despatched. Only after a second had arrived, along with refilled bowls of pretzels, olives and heavily salted peanuts, could he sit back, draw a deep breath and take in his surroundings.

He'd certainly picked the perfect spot to get the sense of Sorrento. A square fed by four roads, it had a small roundabout in the middle as a token gesture toward traffic control. A steady stream of cars, bikes and small flatbed vans criss-crossed in a mesh of near misses, bells ringing, horns sounding. To put a foot on a brake pedal appeared to be something Italians didn't do.

And then there were the scooters – of every model and vintage imaginable, including a besuited businessman, ultra cool, on a Honda Executive, a young, tanned girl in a yellow bikini on a battered Lambretta, and an old guy in paint-spattered overalls with his crash helmet tucked under one arm. Each was carving their own carefree course through the traffic, each sporting the obligatory chic shades. It was Sorrento in a nutshell, all on parade before him.

On the way back to the hotel, he revisited the gift shop to buy a pair of sleek-looking sunglasses. Over the shoulder of the assistant, a well-stocked shelf of spirits caught his eye. A half bottle of Johnnie Walker Black Label joined the shades in the candy-striped bag.

Parked in the hotel driveway, right in front of the steps, stood a scooter. But not any ordinary scooter. It had a red and cream body, matching cream leather double seat and immaculate paintwork gleaming in the sun. A classic Vespa, from the sixties he would guess. Something went click at the back of his brain. How had he remembered that? Did he once have a machine like this? It was a thing of beauty. It was all he could do not to run his finger along the bodywork. The Rolex read five to four. He took the stairs this time.

Still breathless from the climb, he changed plan once inside his room. Instead of pouring himself a Scotch and installing himself in the chair on the balcony, he placed the bag on the floor and flopped onto the bed. He had just drifted into that hazy zone of half sleep when a loud click startled him. It was a key being turned in the lock. At first, he thought someone was trying his door, only to realise that it was coming from the next room. The door opened, then closed. Done carefully and deliberately.

There were seven slow steps. Patent leather soles on parquet floor.

Silence.

A single muffled word. A woman's voice.

Then a whimper, a groan, a moan, building to a howling frenzy of orgasm.

Silence.

Seven slow steps crossed the parquet floor. The opening and closing of a heavy door.

Sleep was now out of the question, and he took a long, cold shower before heading back out into town. It could have been called Limoncelloville, shop windows filled with bottles of the local tipple of lemon liqueur. Wedded to his whisky, there was no chance of him going near the stuff. What did attract him, however, was the seemingly endless number of small bars and restaurants tucked down the side streets and alleyways. So much so that he decided to book a table at *La Cazzarola Trattoria*, a small family affair – all red-and-white-checked tablecloths – nestled away in a courtyard.

Four hours later, he was comfortably ensconced in a window seat, halfway through a carafe of house red every bit as velvety smooth as the fine wine served at the hotel. Lacryma Christi.

'A very special wine,' the waitress said. 'Produced right here, on the slopes of Vesuvio.'

He'd gone for the set menu and wasn't disappointed – *prosciutto e melone, spaghetti alla vongole, tiramisu* – after which an espresso in a tiny cup accompanied by a large *Vecchia Romagna*. Followed by another. For the first time since waking up on a plane beside a chicken, he felt relaxed. This was good. Very good…

The heady scent of bougainvillaea hit him before he reached the hotel. Out front, in exactly the same place, the red and cream Vespa still stood. As he passed, he brushed the worn leather of the seat with his fingertips. It was there to be caressed, so he did…

Another envelope awaited him on the floor of his room. Inside, a brochure of Pompeii together with a handwritten note, unsigned:

The bus leaves at 10.00. Be there!

***

Now he understood. Terracotta roof tiles, whitewashed walls, lemon trees. Now he got it! From his seat at the front of the open-topped bus, he had the perfect bird's-eye view down into the gardens of the villas lining the road. Each immaculately cared for, with one thing in common – a lemon tree. Or several lemon trees.

The bright yellow of the swollen fruit stood out in stunning contrast against the shiny blue glaze of ceramic pots and patio tiles. Suddenly, all the brash-coloured earthenware in the gift shop windows made total sense. Maybe he would even give the limoncello a go. Strictly for research purposes, of course.

It was just as well he'd bought the sun hat and shades. It was going to be a scorcher, the heat haze already building over the bay. At frequent intervals, the road signs told him how many kilometres it was to Pompeii. He didn't need the road signs. They were closing in on the volcano…

The coach park was already filling up, each 72-seater disgorging its gaggle of tourists immediately identifying themselves loudly as either Japanese or American as they poured out onto the hot tarmac. He held back, not wishing to find himself locked into the company of his hotel party. Instead of heading straight for the entrance, he strolled over to the terminus building, where he bought a chilled bottle of still water.

The pressing hordes were funnelled into a short incline up towards the *Porta Marina*, one of the original main gateways on the city wall. In a weird way, he enjoyed the physicality of the queue as it shuffled through the bottleneck and through the turnstile. Bodily contact with other human beings had, somewhere along the way, disappeared from his life.

Three things struck him when he finally entered the town. One, the sheer scale of the place – he was expecting something much smaller. Two, how remarkably intact the incredible buildings were – he was expecting a few remains surrounded by rubble. And three, the dogs. He wasn't expecting the dogs at all. Almost everywhere he looked, they lay in silence in the shade of the walls, tongues lolling. Although strays, they appeared good-natured and cared for.

Over breakfast, he'd thumbed through the neat little *Brief Guide to Pompeii* and picked out a couple of things which pricked his interest. Like the dogs, he didn't want to be out in the sun longer than necessary, so he headed straight along the *Via Marina*, stopping only to marvel at the smooth furrows left by cartwheels in the stone road. A ghostly stillness lay over the deserted street. Apart from the dogs, there was no sign of life. It was as if the turnstile swarms had vanished into thin air.

Having convinced himself that it would not only be morally acceptable but also culturally enriching to study the erotic friezes of Pompeii's number one tourist attraction, the main brothel, he turned left into *Vicolo del Lupanare*, meaning 'Street of the Wolf's Den'. In Latin, she-wolf was evidently the term for a prostitute. But where was everybody? He soon had his answer.

Jam-packed into the narrow street like sardines in a tin was an unhealthy coming together of oriental early teens – all shrieks, bubblegum and ponytails – and elderly Midwesterners – all drawl, white socks and varicose veins, the two groups bonded by the common purpose to take photos of fellatio and cunnilingus to drool over back home. No, on second thoughts, this wasn't for him.

Frustrated that his plan for the day had fallen at the first hurdle, he parked himself on a kerbstone in the shade and flicked open the booklet. A stapled insert advertised a special exhibition – on loan from Naples Museum – of the figures of those who had died in the eruption. The very thought of what had happened there made him dry in the mouth, so he uncapped his bottle of water. As he raised it to his lips, he almost choked…

Standing right beside him was a large dog. A large, female dog. Some kind of Alsatian cross, he guessed, with a sleek, reddish-brown coat. She was beautiful. Maybe she'd heard him open the bottle and had come for water. He poured some in the cupped palm of his hand. She ignored his offer. Instead, she pointed her nose in the air to sniff the hot breeze blowing down the hill.

There was every reason not to stroke her but he could not resist, letting his fingers run lightly across the soft, lustrous fur of her back. He decided to call her Sheba. She allowed his touch without looking at him. *In that moment, he had never felt closer to any other living thing in his life.* She granted him her presence. That was enough. She let out a nostril sigh, then padded away up the hill. He sat and watched her go. She turned round to look him in the eye. He stood up and followed.

She took him for a short walk up to the Forum, across its open, dusty expanse to the door of the *Olitorium*, the indoor marketplace. More morgue than market, it now exhibited the remains of those who perished in the eruption. The dog flopped down in a shady spot by the entrance. He stepped inside. There was quite a crowd clustered around the metal and glass cabinets housing the bodies, so he took time to study the information board first.

He read how Vesuvius erupted the very next day after the residents of Pompeii had been celebrating Vulcan's feast day, hoping to win the favour of the mighty smith god who laboured at his forge inside the mountain. When the volcano blew, a cloud of smoke, ash and toxic vapour blanketed the city, killing at least 2,000 people instantly. The residents who had decided to stay put met their end when the pyroclastic hurricane barrelled over the city wall at over 100 miles per hour.

He read how the bodies of the victims remained in the same position as when the blast hit them and, being then covered by the layers of ash, which continued to fall on the city, the form of their bodies were perfectly preserved, even after their flesh and organs had decomposed.

He read how an ingenious archaeologist, on discovering the skeletons, filled the void around the bones with plaster of Paris, making a cast to capture the exact position and pose of the victims' last moments. The huddle of tourists must have all been from the same coach party, as they all suddenly left *en masse*. He'd read the script, so he should have been prepared for what he saw, but so shockingly realistic were the figures that he let out a gasp; men, women, small children, frozen in their death throes. The most striking exhibit was of a grown man who was trying to lever himself up from a lying position, arm raised to protect his face. He had to step back. He wanted to leave this place. And yet, something held him there. In the far corner, set aside from the others, stood a cabinet with a smaller cast inside. He slowly walked over, heart in his mouth…

It was the body of a dog, grotesquely contorted, mouth wide open, teeth bared. The board told him that it was a guard dog, belonging to a Marcus Vesonius Primus. It was tethered to a post in the atrium of the house when the blast struck. As the red-hot cinders rained down through the opening in the roof, the *compluvium*, and started to build up in the passageway, he scrambled on top of them, twisting himself with his back to the ground and his legs raised upwards, wrenching his neck in a frantic attempt to tear himself free. As the chain was stretched to its limit, he was choked and buried alive by the ash.

And what of his master, the wealthy Marcus Vesonius Primus? There was no record of him being found in his house. No doubt, a man of his means would have been one of the first to hurry down to the harbour to make good his escape, leaving his dog to die the most horrific death imaginable. The bastard! With tears in his eyes, he headed for the exit, the bright sun blinding him as he stepped out into the daylight. The dog with the reddish-brown coat was nowhere to be seen.

His original plan to spend the whole day there was now out of the question. All he wanted to do was get out of the place and never return. Luckily, he managed to flag down a bus just as it was leaving and, within half an hour, he was back in Sorrento.

**

Having consigned all thoughts of further excursions to the bin, he spent the week drifting between the pleasurable constants of hotel, bars, cafes and restaurants. Walk a bit. Sit down for a coffee and cake. Watch the world go by. Walk a bit. Have lunch. And so on… Not forgetting, of course, the daily 4 o'clock sexual sound show broadcast from room 47.

A common weapon in the armoury of the thief listener is the glass against the wall. He didn't need one. If anything, she was becoming louder by the day. Like a carefully rehearsed dance routine, the precision was uncanny.

Door clicked open and closed.

Seven steps across floor.

Silence.

Pulsing orgasm.

Silence.

Seven steps across floor.

Door clicked open and closed.

Silence...

As his breathing deepened, it occurred to him that if Vesuvius were to erupt again to cover the whole of Sorrento in ash and his current body pose was captured in perpetuity in a glass cabinet as a tourist attraction, his *in flagrante delicto* plaster cast would be the most visited of all.

That evening, back at *La Cazzarola*, he amused himself by attempting to set out all the possible scenarios of what was going on in the room next door:

1. Woman has male lover who leaves his place of work at 4 o'clock each afternoon to pleasure her...
2. Woman has female lover who leaves her place of work at 4 o'clock each afternoon to pleasure her...
3. Woman hires male gigolo for 4 o'clock each afternoon.
4. The *Tramontano* offers a bespoke package for residents with particular needs. His thoughts moved to the hotel's male members of staff. The dark-haired young beau on front desk? The muscular porter with the moustache? Old Bloodhound? Noooo...!
5. Woman enters room. Woman masturbates. Woman leaves room.
6. Old American tourist brings photos of erotic scenes from Pompeii...

No, stop! This was getting silly.

After one too many large glasses of earthy red and two too many glasses of *Vecchia Romagna*, he paid the bill and tottered out of the trattoria. On entering the hotel grounds, he burst into song:

> *Auntie Mary*
> *Had a canary*
> *Up the leg of her drawers.*
> *When she farted,*
> *It departed*
> *To a round of applause.*

God, how he was enjoying himself!

> *Auntie Mary*
> *Had a canary*
> *Up the leg of her drawers.*
> *When she farted,*
> *It departed*
> *To a round of applause!*

***

Thursday. One day to departure. London Heathrow, it said on the ticket. And then? Whoever was looking after him had done a pretty good job of it so far, so why should he worry? Even so, he felt a gnawing anxiety about what might be heading his way next.

A late morning dip had become part of his daily routine, a couple of leisurely lengths before chilling in the shallow end, where the pool had been cleverly moulded to form a row of underwater loungers. From there, he would lie and watch the noisy antics of the swallows, often swooping right above his head to skim the surface of the pool for a drink. Slightly disconcerting, however, was the direct view he had of Vesuvius through the gap between the *Tramontano* and its neighbour. Every time he looked at it, he thought of the dog...

Normally, he had the whole pool to himself, peak period being late afternoon when guests returned hot and dusty from their days out. Today, he had company. A woman with a book, turquoise bathing costume, mid forties, jet-black hair swept back in a ponytail, thick-rimmed reading glasses, serious looking. After a few furtive glances were exchanged, he took the plunge.

'Good morning.'

She looked up and smiled. 'Morning. Lovely isn't it? Are you here for long?'

'Checking out tomorrow.'

'You'll be lucky!' she laughed.

'Sorry?'

'The volcano. Still not the worst place in the world to be stuck, is it?'

'What?' he said, a little too loudly, jumping up from his seat so quickly he nearly lost his trunks. He stood in horror staring at Vesuvius.

'No,' she laughed again, 'not this one. Big eruption in Iceland. Thrown up a massive ash cloud into the atmosphere. Closed down all flights across Europe.'

'Oh, right...' He sank back into his chair, letting her words sink slowly into his brain. What she was saying seemed so surreal. One thing was clear, however, Sorrento was not the worst place to get stuck in.

'Yep, looks like we're all stranded here together,' she added, removing her thick-rimmed reading glasses.

Could she be the Woman in Room 47?

At her impromptu ops centre in the Grand Salon, Citalia Gina was under siege, without backup. It had begun calmly enough. She explained that, due to the ash cloud, their scheduled flight from Naples was cancelled and that, at this stage, there was no confirmation of when the next flight would be. As the *Tramontano* was fully booked, they would be transferred to the *Renaissance* hotel in Naples and Citalia would cover the initial cost of accommodation. This simple statement triggered a tsunami of questions from the floor, none of which she was in a position to answer:

'How much compensation is Citalia going to pay us for this fiasco?'

'I have an unused ticket for the Limoncello Distillery. Can I exchange it for a ticket to the Naples Museum?'

'Can you guarantee our in-flight meal order for one gluten-free and one vegan will be transferred to our new flight, whenever that is?'

Gina brought the meeting to a swift close with the promise of more envelopes slipped under doors to confirm departure arrangements. The gathered assembly dispersed, only to reform in small huddles in the foyer, much to the annoyance of front desk.

'I just have to get back to the office. The place will collapse without me.'

'My employer will dock me pay for any days lost, the twat!'

'My wife thinks I'm at a counselling conference in Cleethorpes...'

***

A cloud-laden sky matched the mood of the coach, a coach full of unanswered questions. For the majority it was how will I get home and when will I get home? For the man named as Colin Barker in his passport, the question was more fundamental. Where is home? He was already wishing he were back in Sorrento. He could have happily stayed there for the rest of his days. From the conversations around him, he gleaned that an unpronounceable Icelandic volcano had spewed clouds of ash up into the atmosphere, grounding all European air traffic because of the risk of debris being sucked into the planes' engines. No one knew how long this would carry on. Basically, they were fucked.

Their first impression of Naples on the ride from the airport had been of a city which was crowded, edgy and slightly intimidating. As the coach inched its way into the centre, they had time to observe it at closer quarters as a city which was crowded, edgy and more than slightly intimidating. Grey Shoes did nothing to lift their spirits.

'Bloody Naples! Let's only hope they give us a room with a safe!'

A far cry from the elegance of the *Tramontano*, the hotel was a modern, marble-clad building, enclosed by soulless office blocks. To add to the misery, it started to rain. While everyone pushed and shoved to retrieve their suitcases, the man stood transfixed. Parked outside the front of the hotel stood a scooter. Not just any old scooter, a red and cream Vespa. There was no mistaking it. Repressing the strong urge to walk over and brush the raindrops off the tan leather seats, he waited to grab his case and followed the others up the hotel steps. Inside, it looked like they'd just finished a major refurb. Clean lines of dark wood, steel and glass with bright green decor. Gina had herded the group into the spacious bar area.

'Welcome to the *Hotel Renaissance*.' She would be based at the airport, she said. At the moment, it looked like they would be there for at least three days, she said. She would return to the hotel at six to give an update, she said. Cleverly, she closed by saying that the rooms were now ready. So, instead of hitting her with a barrage of questions, complaints and worse, the party stampeded to be first in the queue at reception. In spite of the fact that they were going to be there for the foreseeable future and had nothing planned for the rest of the day, it was as if their lives depended on getting to the front of that line.

When it finally came to his turn, all he could do was stare open-mouthed at the key the girl handed to him.

Forty-eight…

The room itself was more than presentable – new, light oak furniture, flat-screen TV, more bright green decor. French windows opened out onto a Juliet balcony, from where he had the perfect view of the sheer, black marble frontage of a bank. Directly below, in a doorway, sat an old woman in a black cowl. Before her, a mat on which rested a begging bowl and a white stick. Beside her, a dog.

Down in the bar, a small group had gathered, without drinks. Barker ordered a *Nastro Azzurro*. Amongst them, the usual suspects – Grey Shoes and wife, the hardy trekkers and the young tweedy couple with the boys. Their younger son was transfixed by the bowl of pretzels and peanuts the waiter had brought with the beer. Barker ushered it to the centre of the table. An Arsenal-shirted older man was speaking.

'Look, the girl said they haven't a clue when the next flight's going to be. There's got to be other ways to get back to Blighty. Train, coach…'

'Coach?' groaned a young woman next to him. 'That would take days.'

'You're right, but if we left tomorrow, we'd be home for Monday.'

Grey Shoes chipped in. 'I propose we split up, find out what options are open to us, and report back here in the bar at five.'

'Good idea,' said one of the trekkers. 'We'll take the coach station.'

A young couple piped up, 'And we'll take the train station.'

The waiter had given them up as a lost cause and returned to drying the same glass on a towel. Above his head, a large, flat-screen TV showed aerial footage of the ash cloud, switching to images of chaotic airport lounges, then back to the volcano, which was showing no signs of abating.

'June and I will pay the British Consulate a visit,' said Grey Shoes. 'I'm sure they'll be on the ball. So, guys, we'll reconvene here at five, OK? Good luck, everyone!'

And so it was that the Great British Escape Committee, Naples Branch, was formed...

***

What on earth possessed him to join them, he'd never know. Maybe he found them fascinating in some strange way. Maybe he just didn't want to be on his own.

'My name's Trevor, and this is my good lady, June. We hail from Halesowen,' he added, with pride.

A simple handshake, that was all that was offered. A courtesy. A gesture of greeting. But he couldn't do it. Instead, he pretended to have something in his eye.

'Sorry! I'm, er, Colin. Colin... Barker.'

'Pleased to meet you, Colin. Are we fit to go now? Do you need the loo, June?'

'No thank you, I do not,' she glowered.

'Oh, it's just that you usually...'

'I do *not!*' she hissed.

'Righty-ho.' Trevor consulted the device which appeared welded to his palm. For some reason, he referred to it as a blackberry. '*Via dei Mille 40*. It's right in the centre.'

'I'll get a map,' said Colin.

Once away from the couple, he was tempted to head straight up to his room and lock the door behind him. What was he thinking? The man was clearly a prick of the highest order. His conscience got the better of him and he picked up a street map of Naples from reception before joining them outside. An instinctive glance at the scooter bay drew a blank. Gone too from the doorway across the street was the old, blind beggarwoman.

A couple of blocks' brisk walk and they found themselves on the *Via Toledo*, a busy main thoroughfare. People spilled out of the shops onto the already crowded pavements, where street vendors stood in their way at every turn.

'This way, shortcut,' he blurted, darting down a cobbled side street. The couple followed without question, only too happy to leave the maelstrom behind. Outside a trattoria sat a large table of old men, identically clad in black suits with white shirts, playing cards. A powerful mix of cigar smoke and strong coffee aroma hit their senses as they passed.

'Look, Trevor!' said June, pointing ahead. 'It's just like one of those Italian beer adverts on the telly.'

Heavily laden washing lines zigzagged the street, from

balcony to balcony. Two women paused their cross-street chatter to look down at them, ignoring Trevor's half wave of greeting. A baker's van was parked ahead, the driver winching up a wicker basket covered by a red-checked cloth up to the top floor. The street took a sharp dog-leg to the left and sloped downwards quite dramatically. The traffic noise dimmed to a distant hum until the only sound they could hear was the echo of their footsteps.

'Can we turn back, Trevor? This doesn't feel right.'

'I say, old boy, are you sure you know where we're going?'

'Yes,' he lied.

A flight of steps took them further down to a small, empty square, dank and dark. The diminishing segment of bright blue high above them spoke of another world, a world which they had left behind in a matter of minutes. Then, from behind them, came the sound of footsteps.

'Trevor, I'm scared.'

'It's alright, darling,' said her husband, unable to control the tremor in his voice.

The man going under the name of Barker wasn't scared. *No, he'd experienced worse. Much worse...*

'Come on!' They took the next alley on the left, so claustrophobically narrow that their shoulders brushed the walls on either side. As the following footsteps quickened, so did theirs.

And then, from nowhere, the underbelly of Naples spat them out into the glaring brightness of a huge *piazza*, loud with life. It was as if they were reborn into another world, a world with the unmistakable stench of rotting fish, having arrived bang slap in the middle of a bank of stinking waste bins at the back of a seafood restaurant. They squeezed their way through to stand, breathless, next to a scooter rank.

'There, you see, darling. Colin knew the way all the time.'

Darling fixed the two men with a stare as cold as a limoncello lolly on a winter's day.

From there, the consulate was easy to find, housed on the top floor of an elegant building set back from the main drag. Hearts sank as they saw the queue snaking out into the gardens. It took them well over an hour to reach base camp, a cramped reception housing three chairs, a magazine table and a ridiculously large Union Jack at ease in an umbrella stand, probably dusted off and wheeled out to give comfort to the displaced citizenry in their time of need. From behind the glass of the reception desk, a harrowed young woman struggled to offer a thin smile of welcome.

'Good morning!' said Trevor. 'Could you possibly brief us on Her Majesty's government's plans to evacuate its subjects from Naples?'

Evacuate? Did he think a warship was going to be diverted from manoeuvres in the North Atlantic to act as cruise liner for a couple of hundred tourists?

The woman on reception sighed with her eyes. 'Good morning, sir. As you may know, it is as yet unclear when flights will be able to resume. Are you on a package trip?'

'Yes, but…'

'Our advice at present is to liaise with your travel company…' Grey Shoes opened his mouth to speak, '…but as a contingency, we have ordered a fleet of coaches which are leaving the UK for Europe tomorrow. Two coaches are expected to arrive here on Tuesday at noon.' Trevor opened his mouth to speak again, but she headed him off at the pass by thrusting a single sheet of paper into his hands. 'Tickets are 150 euro each. Would you like to purchase now?'

'Er... we'll have to think about it.'

'Thank you, sir. Enjoy your stay. Next please!' By the look on her face, she couldn't wait to return to the normal fare of lost passports, stolen handbags and stabbings.

'Maybe the others will have better news,' said June, once they'd squeezed their way down the narrow staircase and out of the front door. 'Don't you think we should have bought the coach tickets, just to be on the safe side?'

'Absolutely not. We'll be out of here sooner than that,' her husband replied, removing a black leather wallet from his pocket. 'Remember, darling, I have the company's Barclaycard Platinum. This little beauty will open doors.' She didn't look convinced. She didn't want any doors opening. She wanted a ticket back home. 'So, we might as well do a spot of sightseeing, while we're here. Would you care to join us, Colin?'

'No,' he replied, far too quickly.

'Er... would you mind terribly if we took the map?' June blurted, clearly still traumatised by the memory of dark alleys and washing lines.

'Of course. Have a nice day.' He watched them leave, arm in arm. Barclaycard fucking Platinum...

He spent the afternoon wandering from shaded *piazza* to shaded *piazza*, grazing on *gelato* and *espresso*. Turning into a side street, he almost bumped into the Tweed family, noses pressed against the glass of a shop window. Curious, he crossed the road and sidled into an arcade to observe more closely. They were at a fast-food outlet called SpudULike. Why on earth would they be wanting to eat some franchised American crap when they had all the Italian delights of a hundred and one trattoria to choose from? And baked potatoes, in this heat? With a shake of his head, he moved on.

His route back to the hotel took him across a large square dominated by an imposing public building, in front of which stood a line of demonstrators with placards. Their half-hearted chants echoed across the largely empty expanse. At the foot of the steps stood a line of armed riot police, accompanied by a water cannon. Neither side looked as if they wanted to be there. So engrossed was he in the stand-off, that he almost stumbled into the Tweeds sitting on a stone bench.

'Oh! Hello…' he stuttered.

'Hello,' the woman smiled.

His eyes went to her lap. On a paper plate, she was dissecting a small baked potato into four pieces with a white plastic knife. Now he understood. The hungry looks of the boys in the hotel bar, the noses pressed against the takeaway window. It was hunger. He knew that look. They had been looking for the cheapest warm meal they could find. They had run out of money. Aware of the wad of notes in his wallet, his immediate instinct was to offer them a loan to tide them over until they could return home. An inner voice held him back. *You are not here to help them*, it said. He mumbled an embarrassed farewell and headed back to the hotel.

Thoughts of the large double bed awaiting sped him on his way – he'd seen enough of the streets of Naples for one day. Besides, a quick look at the Rolex told him it was getting close to four. Without realising it, the demonstration was taking place just round the corner from his hotel. It was ridiculous, he knew, but a sliver of hope wanted the magnificent machine parked outside to belong to the Woman in Room 47. It was ridiculous, he knew, but a sliver of desire wanted her to be occupying the room next to his. He bounced up the steps.

Four o'clock passed. He was stood up – left high and dry. In spite of his silent prayers, there was no second coming. Instead, a nightmare awaited, in which he found himself writhing about naked with Wallpaper June in a large wicker basket being winched up to a balcony, with Trevor – also naked – leaning over the balustrade to take pictures.

***

So soundly had he slept that he almost missed the inaugural meeting of the Escape Committee. Grey Shoes was brandishing his copy of yesterday's *Daily Mail*.

'We've made the front page, folks!' he declared. Dear god, came the collective sigh. He's now going to read the bloody article out loud to us. Colin threw a desperate look in the direction of the bar, but he need not have worried – the waiter was already headed towards him, a top-heavy designer glass of *Nastro Azzurro* balanced expertly on his tray.

'Incredible, don't you think, guys? Whole economies ground to a halt. For a week, or even more! Millions of people unable to go to work. We won't see anything like this in our lifetimes. And just to think – we were there! That'll be one to tell the grandchildren.' He paused to take a sip from his Martini.

'We don't have any bloody grandchildren,' muttered his wife, at no one in particular. Then, directing a fierce stare at her husband, she snarled, 'Because, in case you hadn't noticed, Trevor, we don't have any children.' The woman in the wallpaper dress downed her daiquiri in one. Undeterred, Trevor went on to feed back on the comprehensive support package Her Majesty's government had put in place.

'Next Tuesday?' cried one. 'The flights could be back on by then!'

'I could walk home by then,' added another. A little miffed at the response to his presentation, Trevor retreated to the solace of his Martini.

'Talking of coaches,' piped up the Arsenal shirt, 'there was a Romanian guy here earlier. They have coaches leaving on Saturday and they could pick us up from the hotel.'

'To England?'

'Almost. To Calais, then we could get the ferry.'

'Sounds good.'

'Ah, but there is a catch. It's not cheap. It's 300 euros a seat.'

'Outrageous!'

The rangy backpacker, introducing himself as Nicholas, said, 'And we should be careful, here. They will more likely than not be unlicensed opportunists, probably uninsured. Or even worse, part of an organised crime network. And will there even be toilets on the coach?'

The consulate's offer suddenly recovered a notch or two. So much so, that Trevor took the opportunity to reclaim the role of unelected chairman.

'So, how about the trains?'

The young couple laughed nervously before the boy, Troy, began. 'It was sheer bedlam at the station. Must have been over a thousand there. Took us over an hour to actually get into the building. And then the queues, you'd never believe...' A sharp dig in the ribs sped his report on to its recommendations. 'Oh, er, yeah. The trains seem to be running as normal and the best bet is to buy a ticket to Torino, then change to Paris for Calais or, alternatively, to Barcelona.'

'Barcelona?'

'Yes, people in the queue were saying there were still flights operating from there to Shannon in Ireland.'

'How come?'

'Something to do with prevailing winds from the Gulf Stream keeping the route clear of the cloud.'

'But that could change?'

'Er, yes, I suppose so,' he said, a look of panic spreading across his face. They'd clearly bought two singles to Barcelona.

The tweedy father with the two little boys stepped into the silence. 'Well, that's good, isn't it? We have some options, at least. And Gina may have some news for us at six.' His wife nodded in support.

With tears in her eyes, June suddenly blurted out, 'If only we knew what was happening! I can't bear all this uncertainty. I can't bear not knowing what's going to happen from one minute to the next.'

'Welcome to my world, darling.'

'Well I don't want to be in your fucking world, Trevor!'

The mother of the two boys covered the younger one's ears in case more was to come. She need not have feared, as the woman stormed out, knocking over a stool in the process. Trevor looked at Colin, rolled his eyes to the heavens and mouthed, 'Time of the mump.'

Time of the mump? What the hell was he on about? Did she have mumps? No wonder she was in a bad mood. But wasn't it contagious? The waiter glided over to right the stool with an ease of movement born from years of experience. The group fell silent, each deep in thought as to what their next move should be. Colin had no such thoughts and ordered another beer.

Right on time, Gina entered the foyer, followed by a gaggle of guests who'd pounced on her as soon as she'd pulled up outside, like a hungry pack of *paparazzi*. Taking up a position against the far wall of the bar, she cleared her throat and waited for the hubbub to subside.

'As you will have seen on the TV coverage,' she began, 'the Eyjafjallajökull volcano is still producing a dense cloud of ash which has spread across most of Europe. I'm afraid, therefore, that the situation remains unchanged. The threat of volcanic debris causing damage to aeroplane engines remains high, so the aviation authorities have ordered that all flights remain grounded until further notice.'

Groan, carp, mumble, mumble, swear. 'So is there a chance that we're still on for next Tuesday?'

'I would say that seems highly unlikely as it stands, but I will obviously keep you informed of any developments. Now...' she cleared her throat again, 'Citalia will, of course, honour your return flight, whenever that is. As far as the hotel is concerned, however, we will cover your accommodation here at the *Renaissance* up to and including Sunday night.'

'But that's the day after tomorrow!' howled the crowd.

'Yes, I know. But, I do understand the hotel does have rooms vacant, if you decide to stay here. I advise you to contact your travel insurance companies to check your situation. Remember, there are no incoming flights, so there should also be plenty of rooms available in the city at other hotels. As I said, I'll let you know as soon as anything changes. Otherwise, I'll be back here at six tomorrow.' Wisely, Gina didn't wait for questions.

Some made a beeline for reception, some went straight up to their rooms, and others stood in couples demanding to know of their partner why the fuck they hadn't booked the travel insurance. After a while, the lobby began to clear, leaving two large orange rucksacks propped up against a leaflet stand. Stephanie and Nicholas were checking out at reception. Of all in the group, they had seemed the most clear-headed and sensible. It wouldn't have surprised him in the slightest if they were about to set off to walk the whole way back home. He chuckled. The exodus had begun…

The man with the lager remained seated. Should he be worried, he asked himself. After all, he had no family, no home, no job to rush back for, did he? The bulging wallet in his hip pocket told him he had enough cash to sit this out. So why worry? The answer was clear. Everything had been laid on a silver platter for him, as if he'd won some surreal mystery jackpot – best hotel room in town, special table on the terrace, suitcase full of new clothes, walletful of readies. All he'd had to do was sit back and enjoy. But things were about to change, he sensed, for the worse. One by one, his kind would be deserting him. He was going to be left on his own again.

The prospect of a return to solitude chilled him to the bone. The ice-cold lager in his hand now felt so unbearably cold that he put it down unfinished on the table, left a tip for the waiter and headed up to his room. Hardly had his head hit the pillow before he plunged into a deep sleep, tumbling into a nightmarish other world of cages, tunnels and handlers.

It was the unmistakable, throaty engine roar which woke him. He sat bolt upright and stared through the window at the darkness outside. The Rolex confirmed it was the middle of the night. Twenty past three? It can't be. Shit! He'd missed dinner! Food was forgotten in an instant as the scooter pulled up outside. He leapt from the bed and ran over to the window just in time to see a slim figure dismount and skip up the hotel steps. Holding his breath for what seemed a lifetime, he finally heard the click of a key in a door. His heart skipped a beat. He'd been right all along! The red and cream scooter *did* belong to the Woman in Room 47 and now she'd moved in next to him again.

But he was wrong. He was so, so wrong. It was his door being opened...

***

She padded across the room and placed a finger to his lips. 'It's praise and reward time, Mr Barker,' she smiled. 'You've been a very good boy.'

There was a wild beauty about her. Deeply tanned skin, reddish-brown hair, street urchin-style. Yellow cotton T-shirt, stretched tautly over her breasts, short denim miniskirt, scuffed leather ankle boots. But it was her eyes – one the deepest amber, the other the brightest blue.

She took his hand. 'Come, we have no time to lose.'

In the lift, she pressed the button for the top floor. As she turned her back to him to look at herself in the mirror, running her fingers through her hair, he stared at the dark sweat line running down her spine. She was giving off a strong, musky scent.

'I have to ask you something. Were you in the room next door in Sorrento?'

'Indeed I was. And, before you ask, I was alone. Let's call it my undress rehearsal, preparing myself for opening night.

You're not about to get stage fright, I hope.' He didn't answer.

In the middle of the night, the lift doors didn't open to a surge of hotel guests trying to force their way in. No, they were on the eighth floor and quite alone. In the middle of the night, they didn't have to wait at the podium before being escorted to their table. She swept him past the long buffet tables of the Garden Terrace Restaurant, empty and eerie, out into the cool night air. Out over the roofs of the city, lights twinkled across the bay. Straight ahead, if anything even more menacing in the dark, loomed the shadow of Vesuvius. Still holding him by the hand, she led him through the tables, each precision set for breakfast. All except one…

In the far left corner, right up against the balustrade, stood a solitary table, ready and waiting to be laid. The woman with the reddish-brown hair let go of his hand, hitched up her skirt and bent over the table, legs wide apart, hands gripping the edges.

'Fuck me.'

'But… but… I haven't got any protection.'

'You don't need protection. You got me. Now do it!'

'But what if someone comes?'

'That is the whole aim of the exercise, you silly boy. Take me now!'

His little tin soldier had been standing to attention from the very moment she'd entered his room. A whimper left her lips to announce his tentative entrance. He felt himself swell inside her and she did too, letting out a low groan. The squeals of tyres and sounding of horns echoing up from the *Via Toledo* did their level best to drown out her cries, but were no match. She came within seconds, long and hard and loud, with an orgasm so primaeval in its raw intensity it scared him.

She stilled, drawing deep breaths through her nostrils. 'Well done, Barker. You are a very good boy indeed. Now do it again, but harder this time.'

He obeyed, thumping against her buttocks with such force that the table started to scrape a squeaky course across the marble floor.

'Oh, god...' he moaned.

'Come on,' she urged. 'Take me!'

He slowed to a standstill.

'What are you doing? Don't stop now, for fuck's sake, I'm almost there!'

A single word left his lips.

'Chicken...'

Right in front of him it stood, perched on the balustrade, preening its wing feathers. Definitely the one on the plane, it paused to cock a sideways glance at him before returning to matters of body hygiene.

'Don't worry about him, he's with me,' she said, as the chicken stopped cleaning itself and started to move along the stone ledge. 'Concentrate on what you're doing,' she hissed, feeling him soften inside her. She twisted round to get a better view of the bird. 'Will you fuck off, Ferdinand! I'm in the middle of something important here!'

Ferdinand took no notice. Instead, he started to march along the balustrade in a stiff-legged gait, his vivid red crest standing proud. The sight of a goose-stepping chicken killed his erection outright. It was hard enough keeping a straight face, let alone a straight dick.

'Bloody hell,' she groaned, uncoupling herself from him. 'I don't normally do this,' she said, guiding him with her fingertips towards a chair at the next table. 'Sit!' she said, forcing his knees apart. 'There's a good boy.' She knelt before him. 'But understand this, Barker. You don't come into my mouth. Right?'

'Right,' he said, hoping his cock had understood the message. The very thought of what he was about to receive rendered him as stiff as a broomstick in seconds. She leaned forward to cover him with her moist lips. 'Ooh,' he groaned, eyes closed, pressing his hands flat on the table behind him. She was now taking deep breaths through her nostrils, her head slowly bobbing up and down in a smooth rhythm. Cutlery started to rattle, cups clinked against saucers, a small vase of flowers toppled over, wetting his fingers.

He opened his eyes to see a tongue of flame lick the night sky, then came the rumble...

The chicken squawked.

The volcano erupted.

The Barker did both.

***

The scowl said it all. 'I told you not to do that,' came the growl, wiping her mouth on the back of her hand. 'Come on, we have to go.'

This should have been the moment he was lying back in the soft bed of room 48, her head resting on his chest, her slender fingers tracing slow doodles through the hairs on his forearm. Instead, he was hurtling down eight flights of stairs, trying to fasten the buckle on his belt. Halfway down, the fire alarm sounded, bringing bleary-eyed sleepers out onto the landings, only to scatter like wildebeest as the two lions charged through their midst. The Vespa stood waiting, engine ticking over in an impatient throb. How did that happen? He looked round, half expecting to see a chicken in a crash helmet.

'Get on,' she snarled. 'And hold tight!'

He needed to. Feet pressed down hard on the running boards, knees pressed in tightly against the fairing, he bear-hugged her round her waist. His left cheek pressed into her sweat-soaked back, he realised this was the closest he was going to get to a post-coital moment.

The streets were sheer bedlam, each thoroughfare a seething mass of panic and anger. This time the car horns were for real. She carved her way through the city like a knife hacks at a crust of stale bread, throwing the machine into corners, mounting pavements, scraping between stationary traffic. The acrid smell of burning tyre rubber hit the back of his throat, as she ripped through the gears without mercy. She took to the unlit alleyways, swatting aside anything that dared stand in her way – dustbins, bicycles, patio sets.

'Hold tight!' she screamed, just seconds before they plunged down a flight of stone steps, losing one of the wing mirrors in the process. The rear number plate was next to go as she overcooked a sharp bend and slammed sideways into the closed shutter of a baker's.

Finally, miraculously, they made it out of town, more or less intact. He gulped in lungfuls of warm night air, only then realising that he had been holding his breath ever since they'd left the hotel. Braving a look over her shoulder, he saw that they were now on the open road, clear of traffic. All the cars were jam-packed into the opposite carriageway, a slow viscous stream of headlights crawling towards Naples, hell-bent on putting as much distance between themselves and the volcano as possible. Only an idiot would be heading towards it. So what the fuck was she doing?

For the first time, she eased off the throttle to avoid a head-on with an emergency vehicle, klaxon wailing like an ice cream van on steroids. He could feel a low rumble beneath them just as a shower of sparks lit up the sky right above their heads. It felt as if they were under the very volcano itself, and it was about to blow. Undeterred, she forged on, until the smouldering mountain was behind his left shoulder. He allowed himself a sigh of relief that they were finally heading out of the danger zone. But where to?

From the string of lights sweeping round the bay ahead, it looked like they were travelling back to Sorrento. She was taking him to the *Tramontano*! This time, she would not be in the room next door, she would be in his large, fluffy bed. He tightened his grip round her waist and nuzzled into the wetness between her shoulder blades. For the first time since he woke up to find a chicken sitting next to him, he felt as if everything was going to be alright. He felt happy.

The Vespa whined in protest as she forced it down into third and stood on the brake pedal. All hope of sex in Sorrento was dashed as she skidded off the *autostrada*. The exit sign said Pompeii…

She cut the engine to freewheel across the vacant coach park. A pale moon cast a ghostly half-light across the painted white lines and letters on the tarmac, like some ancient hieroglyphic symbols revealed for the first time. Once they'd rolled to a gentle halt, she jumped off and held the scooter upright to ease his unsteady dismount. Then, instead of pulling it up onto its stand, she just let it go to fall with a clatter. Dented, battered and bruised, it lay there, discarded like an empty plastic cup. It looked like this was journey's end.

Without so much as a glance of farewell to her once beautiful steed, she headed toward the *Porta Marina* and he followed. To his surprise, she turned off at the last minute to sail right past, until she reached a section of the wall which was being rebuilt. A temporary mesh fence was in place, guarded by a number of signs he couldn't read. There, she stopped and reached down behind a bush to pick something up, a tool of some sort with long red handles – a wire cutter. All he could do was stand and stare, as she snipped at the metal until she was able to pull back a triangular fold.

'Here, take this,' she said, handing him a small cloth pouch.

He stared at it, nestled in his palm, then back at her. 'What…?' The volcano rumbled.

'Go now. Go!'

He crept through, catching his right cheek on a snag of wire. He turned to the Woman in Room 47. She was gone. He opened his mouth to call out to her, call her name. But he didn't know her name. Without any conscious decision on his part, he began to walk along the smooth paving stones once trodden by Romans two thousand years before. He could feel the eyes of the bakers, the milliners, the women of the night following him from the deep shadows.

On entering the wide expanse of the Forum, he let out a gasp at the ringside seat view of Vesuvius, a tongue of lava now licking down the mountainside. If Christ did enjoy his wine, he would now be shedding tears at the creeping, unstoppable incineration of the vintage vineyards. Lower down, a thread of pinprick headlights wound its way down the slope, amongst them, the flashing yellow light of an emergency vehicle. *How could they be so stupid?* he asked himself. How could anybody be so stupid as to build houses on the side of a volcano? And now it was all going to happen again. History repeating itself. He sat down on a fallen pillar to gather his thoughts. Why had she brought him here?

A dark shape glided from the shadows. His heart skipped a beat, thinking it was her, but he was wrong. The dark shape padded up to him, nuzzled against his shoulder, then licked clean the cut on his cheek. It was Sheba, she of the reddish-brown coat. The human was allowed to stroke the dog, her fur silky soft to the touch.

'It is time,' she said. 'Come.'

Not for one second did he question the fact that the dog was speaking to him, but followed her until they reached the door to the *Olitorium*. He stepped forward to the casements – trying not to look at the contorted figures inside – took the pouch from his pocket, opened the drawstring and poured the dust into his palm. It was hot to the touch. He rubbed his hands so that his fingers were completely covered in a red film.

First, to the dog. Tears poured down his cheeks, as he relived the poor creature's final horrific moments. The casing's ring nuts gave easily to his pressure. And so, to the human cast. Just as easily, he removed the glass vitrine to expose the death throe, an arm reaching out, reaching out for someone, reaching out for something.

And then, in that moment, he understood. The man was the merchant *Marcus Vesonius Primus*. Yes, he was a rich bastard, but no, he had not made good his escape from the harbour in a vessel his wealth afforded. Instead, he had turned back to rescue his dog, Tiber, only to be caught by the blast a matter of metres away from his beloved friend.

Even though the cast was heavy, he carried the guard dog across to its owner. As if clicking the final, long-lost piece of a jigsaw into place, he locked their bodies together, their stiff limbs dovetailing in a tight embrace. The hound's nose nuzzled under its master's chin.

Stepping outside, he was stopped in his tracks by the sight of the dogs of Pompeii filing into the Forum until their numbers were so great that they filled the whole square. They had come to bear witness.

The volcano stilled.

A flurry of warm ash drifted down like the first innocent snowflakes of winter, with little hint of the harshness to follow.

His work was done.

A sudden sound from the *Olitorium* made him turn, the blood freezing in his veins as he heard the powerful jaws of *Canis lupus familiaris* ripping into the brittle plaster cast throat of *Homo sapiens*...

1957...

I shouldn't have been on the bus in the first place. It was all Stephen Spaxman's fault.

'Mr Youngs! Mr Youngs!' shouted Matron. 'There's been a terrible accident!'

'Stay in your seats!' the headmaster said. The two of them rushed out of the door.

We rushed straight to the windows. Stephen stood in the middle of the playground with an arrow sticking out of his eye. The red feather flight glinted in the sunlight as he turned and stared at us with the one eye he had left.

We all screamed and ran away from the windows. I hid under my desk. Found my Tintin pencil sharpener I'd thought I'd lost. Someone had trod on it.

He'd brought them into school that morning. Showed us the metal arrow tips his big brother Arthur had put on. Never did find out how it happened. Must have shot the arrow straight up into the air. Still made me sick thinking about it.

Lived in Ross Street, he did. Just past the rec, at the top end. The rough end. Hated delivering papers there. Bottom end was OK – *Express*, *Mirror*, *Sun*. Number thirty-seven even had the *Telegraph*. Top end was all *Racing Post* and *Tit-Bits*. Never looked at the *Racing Post* once.

He lived at number nineteen, next to the Sharkey boys.

They had dog shit on the lawn and a Morris Oxford up on bricks.

Bathtub full of coal outside the front door. Council fitted all the houses with bathrooms the month before. Most people filled them with hot water, swished in the Radox and soaked.

Not the Sharkeys. Ripped theirs out. Stuck it in the front yard and filled it with coal.

Fucking arseholes, Dad called them.

Made sure I sat at the front of the bus, on the seat behind Skip. The Sharkeys were mucking about on the back seat, Billy and Tommy, singing Elvis songs.

Feel their eyes boring into the back of my head, I was too scared to turn round. Only agreed to go because Stephen was going. He would have looked after me. It was going to be a long week.

It was all Stephen Spaxman's fault.

***

Journey took forever. Flat fields full of cabbage as far as the eye could see.

Almost dark when we got to the campsite.

Overstrand, they called it.

By the sea, they said.

Had looked through the window for the sea, but it wasn't there – just trees, fields and more trees.

We unloaded and pitched our tents. I was in Kingfisher, the name of my new six.

The driver reversed back down the track, headlights shining in our eyes.

Wished I was still on the bus.

Skip kept looking at his watch. Someone was supposed to be there to open the toilet block. Everyone went behind the trees. I didn't; too scared.

We lit a big fire. We stuck sausages on sticks and drank gritty cocoa from tin mugs.

Campfire burning, campfire burning,
We drew nearer, drew nearer,
In the glowing, in the glowing,
We sang and we were supposed to be merry,
But not me.

I was shitting myself.

Jackets were poked about in the embers around the fire's edge.

Skip said to leave them, wouldn't be ready yet.

I knew mine was ready, because it was burnt black.

Left it, though.

Out of the dark she came.

One minute she wasn't there, next minute she was.

Never seen a bald woman before. Her head was just like a conker, shiny and brown.

Old Enid, she was called. Sat herself down next to Skip as if she owned the place. Turned out, she did.

Slurped down her cocoa, spat into the fire and told stories about shipwrecks, graveyards and ghosts.

And a big, monster dog:

Black Shuck.

She started to circle us, walking behind our backs.

'It's the size of a calf, red eyes wide as saucers,

noiseless as death. All you will hear is the sound of him draggin' his broken chain. Tinkle, tinkle, tinkle… You'll know he's there alright. Make sure you keep them eyes closed, or you'll be gooin' hoom in a box. If you be gooin' out of a night, keep clear of Shuck's Lane. Tha's where he wanders. Shuck's Lane. Overstrand…'

Overstrand, that's where we were! It lived here!

She stopped right behind me. Smelled of stale piss and burnt rubber. I closed my eyes.

'Well, yes,' said Skip, clearing his throat. 'Thank you, Enid. The boys have had a long day. Best be turning in for the night.'

I went to pull my potato out of the fire. It was burnt to cinders.

Everybody stuck close together in the queue for the toilet. Nobody went for a pee behind a tree.

Inside the tent, Tubby Twinn asked whether the flap was tied tight – three times.

I wriggled down far as I could into my sleeping bag and zipped it up over my head. Turned my Pifco on and pretended I was back in my bed, staring through the condensation on the window at the street lamp over in Sedgwick Street. Echoes of a football chant from happy U's fans on their way back from The Abbey.

We're gonna win the league
We're gonna win the league
And now you're gonna believe us
And now you're gonna believe us
And now you're gonna believe us,
We're gonna win the league!

***

Smell of bacon smoke woke us. Clinky sounds of pots and pans and billycans – laughing voices. We tumbled from stale fart stink out into fresh air. Billy Sharkey was standing outside the toilet block running a steel comb through his greasy quiff. His brother must have been inside. All I had to do was keep my head down I kept telling myself. Lie doggo.

Beans were too hard but everybody ate theirs, so I did. After breakfast, Skip banged a ladle against the bottom of a tin pot.

'Right, troop, this morning we shall be going on a hike through the forest. Before we set off, make sure you have placed any valuables you have in your locker.' Everybody rushed off, leaving me standing in the middle of the campsite. I didn't understand the locker bit.

'Well?' said Skip.

'I haven't got a locker.'

'Over there, in the toilet block. Don't tell me you've lost your key already, Raymond?'

'I didn't get a key, Skip.'

'Where were you last night when I gave them out?'

'Don't know, Skip.'

He felt in his pocket. 'Ah, so that explains this one,' he said. 'I thought it was strange I had one left over. Here...' He gave me a key attached to a disc. Red paint mostly peeled off. 'Number 38. Last one. Off you go, Raymond!'

'Thanks, Skip.'

I ran back to the tent to get my purse. Had saved up

five shillings from my pocket money to get presents for Mum and Dad. Most of the boys had come out of the block, so I took a deep breath and went in.

Was worse than I thought; stank of piss and fag ends. One cracked, yellow light bulb hanging from the ceiling. Dirty cubicles with cocks carved on the walls. That's where they'd take me. Debag me. Stick my head down the toilet. Pull the chain.

Locker 38. Set aside from the others, right in the far corner. Didn't really want to put my purse there, it was dark inside. Not the sort of place I'd want to be. No, I wouldn't want to be locked up in there.

Skip liked his war songs. He was a sapper, whatever that was. Didn't talk about the war, though, just whistled the songs.

So we packed up our troubles in our old kitbags and did our best to smile, smile, smile as we tramped through the forest. The Sharkeys didn't sing along, but mucked about at the back doing their Elvis impressions. Looked stupid doing leg wobbles to Vera Lynn.

There'll be bluebirds over,
The white cliffs of Dover,
Uh-huh-huh...

I didn't care as long as they weren't bothering me. Keep my head down was all I had to do.

New socks itchy; kept falling down. Mum had tightened the garters, but said that if she did any more my toes would turn black and drop off.

The track narrowed, so we had to walk single

file through what Skip called bracken. Soaked our shirtsleeves. Then all of a sudden, we heard twigs crack beside us, just a few feet into the undergrowth.

'It's Black Shuck!' screamed Tubby, and we all started to run from the brimstone breath, the red eyes wide as saucers. There was nowhere to run. We were trapped! I was no longer worried about wet wool round my ankles.

'Stop!' shouted Skip. 'It's only the rabbits; it's nothing to worry about. Troop, quick march!'

So we swung our arms in time, happy to follow our leader out of that place. Even though our leader was marching a lot quicker than a normal quick march and kept looking over his shoulder.

We stopped at a clearing, where one of the sixers dished out lunch packs wrapped in foil. I was about to sink my teeth into the Spam sandwich when I saw it – a tiny baby rabbit, hopping around, but bumping into tree trunks. Its face was all puffy with a milky goo coming out of its eyes.

'Don't go near it!' said Skip. 'It's got the mixie, a rabbit disease. Can't be cured. Spreads like wildfire, they'll all have it.'

Burst into tears, I did. Couldn't help it.

They were onto me in a flash, the Sharkeys:

He ain't nothin' but a hound dog
Cryin' all the time
He ain't nothin' but a hound dog
Cryin' all the time
He ain't never caught a rabbit
He ain't no friend of mine.

Everybody laughed; even Tubby Twinn. He was just glad they'd found their camp victim for the week. All I'd had to do was keep my head down...

We marched on for a long time until Skip gave the command: 'Troop, halt!' We had a drink from our water bottles. The forest floor was covered with sawdust where they'd been cutting trees. We sat on the fresh stumps. Skip said you could tell the age of a tree by counting the rings. That was stupid, so I didn't join in. The trees were dead. How old are you, Mr Tree? Well, I would have been sixty-six next birthday, if some cackhole in a checked shirt hadn't come along with a chainsaw.

Went to sit on a big boulder instead. Wondered what I would find if I cut through that. Fossils of creatures that lived millions of years ago – dinosaurs: triceratops, brontosaurus or iguanodon. How would they feel if I fucked up their rock?

That night in the tent there was no messing about, no talking. It went dead quiet, dead quick. Maybe it was because we were all knackered from the trek. Maybe it was because we all knew it wasn't rabbits we'd heard in the bracken.

Most of my nightmares were the same, a fairground where they have wild animals as well as all the rides. I knew it should be a circus or a zoo, but it's a nightmare fairground, so I can't change it. It's all going OK – wonky mirrors, helter-skelter and candyfloss – until one of the animals, usually a gorilla, escapes and chases me round the tents. I keep falling over, giving up, waiting to be eaten. But every time I stumble, it stumbles too, and we're off again.

Wish I'd had a fairground nightmare that night...

I'm in the clearing, with the tree stumps. I go and sit on the rock. Around me, all the rabbits are running around in a panic – puffy faces, seeping eyes, red-raw ears – bumping into my legs. Then they freeze.

I smell the burnt rubber. Then I see him. Moving out of the forest. Floating on a raft of mist. White mist, black dog, red eyes. But I'm not scared. He hasn't come for me.

The blind bunnies form a line in front of him. Shuck bends his snout down to the first one and bites off its head with a loud crunch. The line of rabbits takes a hop forward. I want to look away, but I can't.

The hound doesn't kill the second rabbit, but leans forward and licks its face, all over, until the last trace of mixie is licked away. He does this again and again, until the last rabbit has hopped away into the trees. Healed, every one of them.

Then he looks at me for the first time. He opens his huge jaws and lets out a terrible howl, foamy slaver dripping from his lips. He bares his fangs and starts to move towards me. I try to run but the rock holds me; won't let me go. He is upon me!

'Aargh!' The massive shape looms over me...

It's Tubby Twinn. 'Wake up, sleepyhead, you'll miss breakfast.'

***

We did miss it. All that was left was burnt bean scrapings from the bottom of the pan. Tasted great! Spent the morning doing knot practice. Had to do six for my Tenderfoot Badge: reef knot, clove hitch, bowline, round turn and two half hitches, sheet bend and sheepshank.

Couldn't get the sheepshank. Stupid knot, anyway. You could see why the others were important – joining ropes together, tightening a guy line, tying a horse to a post so it could be freed easily. But the sheepshank? Bypassing a frayed bit of rope? Use another one! Thing was, I couldn't get the three loops to hold together. I always kept a length of cord in my haversack, so I could practise, but just couldn't do it.

And I couldn't concentrate. All the time I was struggling with the loops, my mind was back in the dream – with the rabbits. And the monster dog. Didn't want to, but knew I had to go back to the clearing...

Got my chance after lunch. Blindfold Tent Pitch; stupid exercise. Why would you cover your eyes to put up a big ridge tent? It was hard enough with your eyes open. Didn't make any sense at all.

It was dead easy to sneak away, 'cos no one could see me. Left them standing with their neckerchiefs tied over their eyes, holding the end of guy ropes looking like gormless statues.

The track through the forest was dark and cold. Shirt soon soaked by the wet bracken. Blinded by the bright sunlight as soon as I came out into the clearing, I wished I'd brought my hat.

Sat on the rock, warm against my bum, I wondered what kind of dinosaurs were inside. Wondered how they'd feel if they knew a little boy sprout was sitting on them. I waited.

One by one, the rabbits came out from the forest. They took a couple of hops, sat up, and looked around. Twitched their ears, looked around again, nibbled the grass. They knew I was there, but didn't mind. Just looked at me every now and then between nibbles. They looked at me from open, clear eyes – no horrible seepy stuff. No puffy faces. They were cured. Black Shuck *had* licked the mixie away!

A twig cracked. The rabbits froze, then scampered back into the trees; disappeared in a flash. The thing that scared them was coming down the track. It was not after them. It was coming for me. I closed my eyes...

'Well, well, well. If it isn't the paperboy,' said Billy Sharkey.

I jumped off the rock to make a dash for it, but his brother was quicker. Grabbed me by the hair and twisted my arm right up my back so it hurt. Billy stood in front of me, legs apart. Took out a steel comb and ran it through his greasy, black hair. Then he swapped the comb for a knife. Not the boy scout one with a bottle opener and a spike for getting a stone out of a horse's hoof. It was a flick knife. He grinned and flicked it open with a click.

'Do you know how to test how sharp your blade is?' he asked.

I did, but didn't say.

'You fold a sheet of newspaper. If it makes a nice clean cut and doesn't tear, then you know it's sharp.'

'So,' said Tommy, wrenching my arm up even further so it really, really hurt, 'if it works on newspaper, it should work on a newspaper boy.' As soon as he said it, he realised he'd stolen his brother's line. That's the problem with having a twin. You think the same things. Wished I had a twin right now, though. He'd come charging out from the trees with a samurai sword swinging above his head and chop them into little bits. But I didn't have a brother – or a sister – so no one came out of the trees to save me.

'He's shaking, the little baby! Shaking like a jelly!'

Billy did his Elvis leg wobble.

> *I said shake, baby, shake,*
> *I said shake, baby shake,*
> *I said shake, baby, shake,*
> *I said shake, baby, shake,*
> *Come on over,*
> *Whole lotta shakin' goin' on.*

When they'd finished laughing, Billy walked right up to me and ran the point of his blade across my cheek, so it scratched the skin.

'You're going to run for me, be my errand boy. Day after tomorrow, when we are all on the Wide Game, you're going to slip away to the store in the village and nick me a packet of fags: Players, Woodbine or Kensitas. None of that filter shit. And no menthol. Got it?'

'Mmm.'

'Leave it under my kitbag in our tent. And don't you dare let your little thieving fingers go wandering. Got it?'

'Mmm.'

He stepped back and his brother let me go.

'And if you tell on me, paperboy, I'll have your guts for garters.'

A branch snapped in the trees.

'What the fuck was that?' cried Tommy.

'Don't worry, it'll be them mixie rabbits.'

They left me, alone in the clearing. I knew it wasn't the rabbits...

***

Came as a big surprise next day when they said we were going to church. Hadn't planned on going back into one of those again. Ever.

Used to be in the choir at St Philip's. Knew all the hymns off by heart. Favourites were 'In the Bleak Midwinter', 'Onward, Christian Soldiers' and, best of all, 'There Is a Green Hill Far Away'. Still sometimes sang them in the bathtub in the kitchen, but didn't go to church no more.

Packed it in after harvest festival last year. We all had to bring something in. Then, when the congregation began to sing 'All Things Bright and Beautiful', each of us had to take the food we'd brought and place it in front of the altar. Marrows, potatoes, carrots, cucumbers and cauliflowers were all laid. And then I went up with my small tin of Del Monte pineapple chunks. The vicar shook his head. Everybody else sniggered. Back in the vestry, they all took the piss.

When I told Dad he said, 'Don't tell Mum.' Then he said, 'That wasn't very bleedin' Christian of them, the bastards.' So I didn't go no more.

But that was only part of it. The main reason I didn't want to go was the story Old Enid had told us round the campfire, about Black Shuck attacking a church in fifteen hundred and something. Scratch marks were still on the door, she'd said, where he'd tried to get in.

The church was much smaller and older than St Philip's. Fourteenth century, Skip said it was. Turned out there were other scout troops there too. One from Overstrand, one from Cromer, and three from somewhere else, at camp like us.

Tubby Twinn was chosen to be our flagbearer, 'cos of his size, I s'pose. Beamed, he did, when Skip strapped the leather harness onto him. Had a brass cup fitted to hold the flagpole. You should have seen him parading up and down the campsite. We all cheered. Proud as punch, he was.

Had put the Shuck story to the back of my mind until the door closed shut with a loud thud behind us. Any minute, I expected to hear the sound of his claws scratching to get in.

Tubby was last in line, concentrating hard on keeping in step. Concentrated so hard on the feet of the bearer in front that he forgot to dip the flag when he got to the rood screen.

'Jesus fucking Christ!' said Skip, as wood met wood, sending a fourteenth-century angel's wing smashing down onto the stone flags.

First thing I did was look for the Sharkeys. They'd be the first to laugh at Tubby. Could only see Tommy at the end of our aisle. Looked round, but couldn't see Billy anywhere. Probably sitting behind a gravestone outside having a fag. Tears were rolling down Tommy's cheeks, but they didn't look like tears of laughter. He was sobbing for real; crying in the chapel.

Knew it was a bad idea going to church. And they didn't even sing any of the hymns I liked. So on the way back to camp, I hummed one to myself.

There is a green hill far away
Without a city wall
Where the dear Lord was crucified
Who died to save us all.

***

Nicking didn't scare me. Didn't want to do it, but it didn't scare me. Done it once before.

It was a Saturday morning. Took the 131 to Drummer Street, then walked through to Boots to buy a present for Mum's birthday. Got her a nice brooch. Crossed the road to Woolies to buy some sweets for the ride back. Stood in front of the pick 'n' mix, looked around, and took a pink shrimp; slipped it into my pocket. Don't know why – just did.

Not once did I take it out. Even just to look at. Stayed there all weekend – in my pocket. From the moment I stole it, I knew it was wrong. Knew I shouldn't have done it.

Knew I had to put it back...

Putting it back was a lot harder. Had to wait until Monday after school. On the bus, kept putting my hand in my pocket, just to make sure it was still there. It had got a bit sweaty and I was worried it might melt.

In the shop, everyone's eyes were on me. I had to

do three circuits of the store before I felt safe enough to stop in front of the sweets counter. Even then, it wasn't easy. Couldn't just take it out of my pocket, stretch forward and place it back into the tub. That would have made everybody look. So I did a little jerky throw from the hip. Trouble was, it went flying all over the other pink shrimps and landed in the sherbet lemons. It couldn't have stood out more, lying there with bits of dark blue pocket fluff stuck all over it. Put my head down and walked out of the store, slow as I could.

'Right, Troop. You know the rules of the Wide Game. Each Six finds a spot to plant their flag in the forest and is allowed to defend it with tripwires, shoulder charges and pea-shooters only. No punching, no catapults, no knives. Understood?'

'Yes, Skip!'

'Off you go then.'

Of course, it was just an excuse for a massive punch-up. Part of me was glad to be out of it, but part of me would have liked to have seen the Sharkeys try to take our flag off Tubby Twinn. Anyway, I had other business to do...

The sign on the gate beside the village store said 'Beware of the Dog'. A black-and-white collie, it was lying down at the bottom of the garden in the shade of a bush. The shop was bigger than it looked from the outside; sold fruit and veg as well as the usual papers, sweets and cards. Checked to make sure there were no other customers inside. Just the one pair of eyes to worry about. They belonged to a fat man. That was good. He wouldn't be able to run fast. Or far.

'Half a dozen Black Jacks, please,' I said.

He looked down at me like I was a piece of shit. 'Tuppence,' he snarled, counting them into a brown paper bag.

Decided I wouldn't mind nicking from him. Handed over the coin, took the bag, and went to leave. Stopped in the shop doorway, just to make sure no one else was on their way in.

'S'cuse me, mister. Have you got a black-and-white dog? It's just chased a car down the road. Nearly got run over.'

'Bloody hell!'

He moved quick for a fat man. Faster than I thought.

'Went round that corner,' I pointed.

Soon as he was out of sight, I was into the shop and behind the counter. Could just about stretch up to the ciggy shelf. Ten Player's No. 6 – that would have to do.

Just got out in time. Fatso was already on his way back, just turning the corner. Stopped in his tracks when he saw me. He looked at me, and I looked at him. Before he had time to shout 'Stop. Thief', I was off.

Then he shouted, 'Stop! Thief!'

I didn't.

Cliff Road was a bad road to choose for an escape – long and straight with no alleyways. All the way down to the sea, it went. Needn't have worried, though. There was no chase. The man was used to kids nicking his stuff and, anyway, all he cared about was his dog. Once he'd found it safe and sound in his garden, that was all that mattered. I reckoned he loved his dog. Must be shit being a shopkeeper, but must be the best thing in the world to have a dog.

Man's best friend, wasn't it?

At the end of the road, I stopped to look over the railing. At last, the sea! Weird that nobody was on the beach, but decided to head down the steep slope to the empty promenade anyway. There was a long line of beach huts, all with their doors closed and padlocked. Painted in different colours. Bright colours – blues and yellows and pinks. All with stupid names. *On The Rocks. Vitamin Sea. Lucy's Shack. Sandy Groyne.*

Parked myself on a bench to catch my breath. Couldn't figure out why nobody was down here on such a nice day. Even the seagulls had disappeared. The wind stilled. The waves stopped rolling in. Didn't like the feel of the place…

'You been doin' somethin' you shouldn't 'ave, boy?'

The voice came from right behind me, from one of the huts. It was a wreck. Peeling black paint, broken windows, didn't have a name. Stood out like a sore thumb. Funny I hadn't noticed it before. The door swung open. There, in the shadows, she sat – the old woman from the campsite.

'You comin' in then?'

Should have scarpered there and then. Don't know what made me go in.

Auntie Gert and Uncle Ern had a beach hut in Caister. Theirs had table and chairs, oil lamp, cupboard for the crockery, checked curtains and everything. This one was bare: bare boards, bare walls and bare, broken window. Not a stick of furniture. She was sitting cross-legged on the floor with her back against the wall.

Tried not to stare at her shiny, bald head, so stared at her bare feet instead – all knotty and knobbly, like they'd been badly carved out of mahogany. Looked round the hut, but couldn't see any sign of shoes anywhere. Sat down in the doorway, so I could make a quick getaway.

She closed her eyes, took a deep breath and sniffed three times.

'Did you believe my tale about the dog? You seen the dog, ain't yer?'

Didn't know what to say. Didn't want to look her in the eyes, so said nothing and kept on staring at her gnarly toes.

'Good on yer. Shouldn't be believin' everythin' you hear or read. Load a bollocks writ about that poor dog. 'Specially the Blythburgh Church story. You read that?'

Looked up and shook my head.

'Arsehole who writ it, nothin' but a publisher. Wouldn't piss on him if he was on fire. Up from London. Needed to make somethin' up to titivate his highfalutin society cronies. Didn't happen like that at all.'

'How do you know?' I heard myself say.

Old Enid ferreted into the folds of her skirts and produced a battered tin, about the same shape and size as a fag packet. She opened it, balanced it on her knees, took a pinch of the bright red powder, carefully sprinkled it on top of her closed fist, leaned forward, and snorted. Her eyes went bright and sparkly.

' 'Cos I was there...' she whispered.

A bony finger and thumb dipped into the tin again to take a second pinch.

'This one's for you. Goo easy, though, it's strong stuff.'

'Is it snuff?' I asked.

'You can call it that if you will,' she said.

So I sat with a bald-headed woman in a beach hut that should have had a name but didn't, sniffing something that should have been snuff but wasn't. I sneezed. And that was when my head exploded...

'Tell me where you are,' she said.

'In the church.'

'Good. Tell me what you see.'

'People in funny clothes. Smocks. Capes. Kneeling. Praying. A boy at the end of the aisle is crying.'

'Tell me what you hear.'

'A terrible howling, coming from outside the door. A scream. Of a boy!'

'What's goin' on now?'

'People are wailing. Now they're running about, screaming their heads off. There's something at the door, trying to break in. I can smell burning!'

'It's OK, it's OK. Goo easy, boy. That'll be the brimstone. Tell me how many people are in the church.'

I started to count. It wasn't easy. Everyone was running all over the place.

'Do I count myself?'

'Oh yes, you are the most important one there.'

It took three goes until I was sure. 'Thirty-eight.'

'There's a good boy.'

There was a loud scratching at the door. I cried out loud.

I was sitting on the sea wall.

I watched a huge woolly mammoth walk out of the

waves, stroll up the shore and melt into the cliff.

I sneezed three times. It was a bright sunny day. The beach was packed. Buckets and spades, sandcastles, windbreaks, kids splashing and screaming in the sea.

I turned round. *There was no beach hut with black peeling paint. There was no old, bald woman.*

***

Don't know how I got back to camp. Went down streets I'd never seen. Took tracks through the trees I'd never trod. All the while, my hand in my pocket, holding the locker key ring with the number 38 on it.

Caught me by surprise when I saw the tents. Almost stumbled into the campsite by accident. Was expecting to be told off. Where have you been? Why didn't you come back with the others? We've been worried sick. But the others hadn't come back. That was the worst thing about a Wide Game; could last all day. No sign of anybody at all. I had the place to myself.

Slipped into Sharkey's tent. Was worried I wouldn't be able to find his kit. Then spotted a small tub of Brylcreem by a sleeping bag. That had to be his. Took the packet of Player's from my pocket and stuffed it into his rucksack. Took the small tub of Brylcreem from beside the sleeping bag and stuffed it into my pocket. Wanted me to be his little thief, didn't he?

I knew what he'd do to me. 'I'll have your guts for garters.' But I didn't care. Crept out of the tent and walked quickly over to the toilet block, hand in pocket again to check my key was still there. Had to stop to sneeze. And again. And again…

Weird. There was a second key on the ring; hadn't noticed that before. Tried it in the door. It fitted. Skip must have given me his master key by mistake. Locked the door and sneaked round the back of the block to take the path to the clearing where we'd seen the rabbits. Where I'd seen Black Shuck in my nightmare. When I got there, I hid behind a clump of bracken, just in case anyone came through on their way back from the Wide Game.

Must have dropped off, because all of a sudden it was dark. I stood up and went over to sit on fossil rock. There were no cries, drifting through the forest, calling my name. No search party with torches. No one had missed me. No one had cared.

It had to happen.

Clink of a chain dragging along the ground. Smell of burnt rubber. Just like in the dream, he floated into the clearing on a carpet of mist. Just like Old Enid had said, his red eyes were as big as saucers.

I was the boy outside the church door. I was the first rabbit in the line. He was now towering over me. I could feel his breath on my face. I bowed my head and closed my eyes. I wished I could say goodbye to Mum and Dad. Just see them one more time…

Suddenly, he let out a little whimper, like he was in pain. I opened my eyes and saw him prick his ears and look up into the sky. There was a bright silver object, right overhead. Too small to be a plane. Too close to be a shooting star. We both followed it until it disappeared over the treetops.

The big hound twisted his head to one side, like he

was trying to figure out what it was. A deep growl gurgled in his throat. He bared his long yellow fangs and let out a blood-curdling howl. A warm trickle of piss ran down my left leg into my sock.

But Black Shuck didn't bite my head off. Instead, he started to whine and nuzzled my side with his massive snout. My pocket. He wanted something in my pocket. The Brylcreem. I took it out and unscrewed the top. He closed his eyes, took a deep breath, and sniffed.

He didn't leave on a carpet of mist. Just turned and padded across the clearing, chain clinking behind, until he disappeared down the forest track.

Towards our camp.

Felt myself trembling. Couldn't stop shaking. Tried to walk about a bit, but didn't help. Finally sat down on fossil rock. Soon as my bum touched the surface, it began to get warm. As the heat rose through my body, I began to feel calm. Like the woolly mammoth, walking out of the sea. So slow, so steady. So calm. Reached down to pull up my pissy sock. It was bone dry.

The first cries sent birds flapping through the treetops in panic. Through all the shrieks and howls, I could make out Skip's voice.

'No, no, no!' he kept screaming.

And then it all went quiet; still as the grave. It was as if the whole forest was holding its breath, waiting for me to get up off the rock and walk down that track. So I did.

On my belt buckle, it says *Be Prepared*.

Nothing could have prepared me for what I saw when I got to the camp. It was like a hurricane had ripped through the place. Guy ropes snapped, tent poles sticking through canvas like broken bones. A torn groundsheet stretched up in the branches of a tree like Jesus on the cross. A beret smouldered in the fire. I stood and listened for any sign of life. There was no one there. The campsite was completely empty. Must have scarpered into the forest, all of them.

And then I saw him.

Sat propped up against the toilet block wall, his wide open eyes staring at me. Two dull marbles, like the one they put in Stephen Spaxman's socket.

Billy Sharkey.

His guts had been ripped open and spilled out on the ground all around him. Yards and bloody yards of them, there were. I'll have your guts for garters, he'd said. Not now, you won't. I make myself stare into the tangled, slimy mess. Staring back at me is the perfect sheepshank. Loop, over loop, over loop.

The toilet door is scratched where he's tried to get in. I open it with my key, step inside and flick the switch. The bare yellow bulb in the ceiling crackles into life. I sit cross-legged in the middle of the floor, take the cord from my haversack and tie the knot. Loop, over loop, over loop.

I know they'll be coming for me soon. So, while I'm waiting, I hum my football hymn.

He died to save us all
He died to save us all
And now you're gonna believe us
And now you're gonna believe us
And now you're gonna believe us
He died to save us all.

THE HIDE

The man smiled to himself as he eased his new hybrid through the twisting curves of the coast road, the first thin rays of dawn sweeping over the expanse of salt marsh to the north. Debussy's 'Claire de Lune' played softly on the radio.

'*We interrupt this broadcast with the breaking news that the serial killer Graham Godber, jailed for life in 1986, has escaped from Woodhill Prison, Buckinghamshire. He is believed to be armed and police are urging members of the public not to approa...*'

At the speed of 40 mph, his stopping distance should have been 36 metres, comprising 12 metres thinking distance and 24 metres braking distance. By reaching down to fumble for the radio button, the man extended his thinking time by a further 8 metres. Two more seconds and he would have hit the body in the road...

He carefully manoeuvred the Lexus round the corpse to park on the verge, climbed out of the car and slowly walked over. It was a dog. Fully grown male who would grow no more. Stiff-legged, eyes wide open.

With some difficulty, he managed to drag it off the road. In his headlight beam, he could see it was a fox red Labrador, one of the designer breeds now fetching over two grand a puppy. At first glance, there was no obvious sign of impact: no trace of the blood, torn flesh and contorted limbs usually associated with a road kill. He knelt beside the body.

'What has happened to you, you poor boy?' he whispered, his hand resting on the silky smooth flank.

There was no collar or tag. The Control of Dogs Act 1992 made it a legal requirement that any dog, while in a highway or public resort, must wear a collar tag that clearly displays the name of the owner, house number and postcode. He knew these things…

'And where on earth are you from?' he heard himself murmur. A blank stare from the empty eyes was all he got in response.

They had company. An impatient caw from across the road announced the arrival of a carrion crow. First course would be the eyes and the man was not about to let that happen. The unused tartan rug was fetched from the back seat of the car. As he reached down to wrap it around the dog's head, he paused.

Something was different. He was sure the empty stare had been cast skyward. Now, the eyes were turned to one side, across the marshes to the sea. No, he must have been wrong. To be doubly sure, he checked again for any sign of life. There was none.

Back in the Lexus, he drew a deep breath. Road Traffic Act 1988, Section 170: Duty of driver to stop, report accident and give information or documentation.

'A driver must stop, contact the police and remain on the scene if they kill or injure a dog.' He knew these things…

But, he reasoned, he had not been involved in the incident which killed the dog. He had merely stopped and removed the body from the road. On the point of contacting the police, he had deliberately left his mobile on the kitchen table. He would use the good offices of the Visitor Centre to make the call later.

The hip flask of Grey Goose in the glove compartment was made for moments such as this. The fact that its top was unscrewed this time every morning was neither here nor there. The car park was only a couple of hundred yards away, so the likelihood of him being stopped and breathalysed was infinitesimal. Two hours out on the marshes should take him back below the legal limit. The man raised the flask to his lips and drank…

***

Awaiting him in the car park was the Land Rover Discovery of Elspeth and Clive. Santorini Black, they insisted on telling him at every opportunity. It was black, for fuck's sake. In the far corner, partly obscured by a drooping buddleia, stood a battered Citroen Berlingo, presumably belonging to another early birder. On its bonnet sat a chicken, preening its feathers. A Rhode Island Red, if he wasn't mistaken. What on earth was that doing here? How odd…

Quite why should the colour of their car irk him today? Quite why should the sleek frontage of the Norfolk Wildlife Trust's Visitor Centre jar with him today? It was the dog, of course. He licked the dry vestige of vodka from the corner of his mouth. Somewhere out there, a family was grieving the loss of their pet. Somewhere out there, a little boy was sobbing his heart out. The little boy inside him fought to hold back a tear. Such was his sense of sorrow that he almost forgot his binoculars. The Celestron spotting scope remained on its tripod in his studio, trained on the bird feeders. Today, he'd decided, would be close-quarter work. Trusty Xenon in hand, he clicked the Lexus locked.

A film of red dust covered the bonnet. As if he didn't believe his eyes, he drew a line with his finger across the paintwork. This was happening more and more. Sahara storms dumping sand over Southern England. Climate change. Of course, Elspeth would have none of it. A wry smile formed on his lips. Let's see how showroom shiny the Santorini Black was now. To his surprise and annoyance, there was not so much as a speck of dust on the Discovery. With a frown, he crossed the road towards the entrance to the reserve. A chill breeze scurried in from the sea.

There, on the gatepost, was attached something which made him stop in his tracks – a small, square sign. No words, just a red circle with a red diagonal line, behind which was a graphic of a dog. A red dog. Unmistakably a Labrador.

'It is not a fox red Labrador,' he heard himself say. How had he not noticed it before? And why not a simple "No Dogs Allowed"? Why did it have to be a red dog only minutes after he'd come across one dead in the road? It was the absence of any other colour on the sign that bothered him most. Red for warning. Red for danger. *Get a grip*, he told himself. There was nothing to be afraid of here…

The boardwalk was meshed with chicken wire against slip hazard. A couple of dragonflies flitted around him, then danced on ahead as if to lead the way. Through a gap in the reeds, across the grazing pastures to the west, the raised causeway from Cley came into view. To think that all of this was once covered by sea. And how long would it be before the waters returned? What would happen to the thousands of migrating birds who found haven here? They would probably be just fine, he mused, far better than the two-legged species which would not be able to adapt so readily.

Within a matter of metres, he was flanked by thickly packed reed bed, soon above head height, the purple flower spikes fanned by stiffening onshore gusts. This was a hidden, secret realm, isolated from the outside world. Enclosed. Cocooned. He felt safe here. Without a shadow of doubt, this was his favourite spot on the reserve, a place where he found himself folded into the close company of warblers and water voles. A sudden ripple of unease swept through the reeds, a swishing uncertainty which brought convicts and carcasses to mind. He quickened his step until he reached the hides, forming a crescent around Simmond's Scrape.

He had almost forgotten that Elspeth and Clive were already there. Clive would have commandeered the furthest bench to the right to get the best view of the pond with the rising sun behind him. That was Clive all over – Gresham's, Balliol, Saracens season ticket holder – and now, a top-of-the-range Discovery in Santorini fucking Black. As for Elspeth, well, there was no knowing where she would be. Maybe in a different hide, maybe up on the shingle bank training her monocular on a great northern diver offshore.

For the second time that morning, a sign stopped him short.

HIDE CLOSED

Birds Nesting
We apologise for any inconvenience
Norfolk Wildlife Trust

'Bollocks,' he muttered, followed immediately by a sigh of regret. It was a bird sanctuary, after all. He knew that the middle hide was already out of circulation for rethatching work, so if another pair had chosen the third as their love nest, then his morning would be wasted.

Thankfully, no more signs were in evidence as he eased open the hide door. As predicted, clad in regulation deer hunter jacket and oilskin hat, a single figure occupied the far right bench, hunched over his spotting scope.

'Good morning, old chap. No Elspeth?' he whispered.

The man in the corner turned to beam a broad smile at him. 'Hey!'

It was not Clive…

***

Flummoxed for a second, he turned to close the door behind him.

'Apologies, I thought you were someone else.'

'Not guilty, Your Honour. Isn't it just awesome here?' he said, loudly.

'Your first time, then?' Eyes already trained on a pair of redshanks, he took up his position at the far end of the bench.

'Sure is. My first day out. Those freakin' quarantine rules of yours, man!' He threw his arms up in despair.

'Self-isolation.'

'OK, whatever. The hotel they put me in was the pits. But this is so exciting, like starting over again.'

The man was breaking all the rules. First and foremost, any talk should be confined to whispers, so as not to disturb the birds – any such exchanges to be restricted to bird-related discussion, without the non-verbal accompaniment of eye contact and body movement. It was a hide, for fuck's sake.

Elspeth would have had him out on his ear by now. Town clerk by name, town clerk by nature, she was a stickler for protocol and etiquette. He wondered where the two had got to. Why had they parked at the Centre if they weren't coming here? Having checked out the redshanks, he swept the Xenon to focus on an avocet, in his view, the most elegant bird on the scrape. It paused mid stride to assess its surroundings, then continued its rhythmic sifting of the mud. He could watch it all day...

The stranger had annoyed him. Far too many birders were too competitive, bordering on the aggressive, for his liking. Only last year, the surprise arrival of a rare rufous bushchat had triggered a frenzy of website alert activity, with scores of sharp-elbowed birders descending on Stiffkey Marshes loaded down with enough camera equipment to kit out Pinewood Studios. And, in doing so, breaching at least three of the Covid rules then in force.

Not for him, the thrill of the chase. While his law school contemporaries made a splash in the shark-infested waters of the legal profession, he had settled for the lapping waves of general practice, rolling up his trousers for the occasional paddle in the shallow waters of a messy divorce or contested will. For some reason, which he still had not quite figured out, this drove his mother mad.

'I had coffee with Fiona Hardwick today. Her Stephen's doing frightfully well at the chambers.' As were David Anderson, Brian Benson, Zack Friedlander. The roll of honour went on...

Home Straight Conveyancing was to become his small but

perfectly formed empire. Two bright young things, Rupert and Jess, attended to all the details and deadlines, while his was the reassuring voice at the other end of the line when offers fell through, chains creaked, surveys surprised. Thanks to the buoyancy of the coastal housing market, business was good – very good. You could keep your murderers, terrorists and sex offenders. He was more than happy with his lot.

'Wow, this is just awesome!' The American shifted his position. There was something which jarred about him. The accent, maybe? He'd once seen *Death of a Salesman* at the Aldwych, the lead role played by an English actor whose American accent was excruciating. Something was not quite right.

The man suddenly looked up from his scope and met his gaze, full on. He had to say something.

'So… where are you from in the States?'

'Iowa. You probably never been there.'

No, but he did know what the state capital was. US presidents, state capitals and nicknames were his responsibility in the pub quiz team, along with politics and classical music. Clive fielded sports, science and flags of the world, while Elspeth took the natural world, literature and food.

'Des Moines,' the man said.

'Oh, right, that's the state capital, isn't it?'

'Sure is. Shithole of a place.'

Whether or not Des Moines was a shithole of a place was immaterial. The fact that the man in the corner could immediately name the city as state capital was enough to allay his concern. Why had he housed those suspicions in the first place?

The avocet paused mid stride, as a pair of quarrelsome

herring gulls made a noisy entrance onto the scrape. Once satisfied that they did not pose a threat, he continued to sift for worms with his fine, upturned bill.

But the nagging doubt would not go away. A stolen glance from the corner of his eye confirmed that the man's jacket and hat were the same make as Clive's. He couldn't be 100% sure, but wasn't the scope a Swarovski Optik, too? Like the one Elspeth bought for him last birthday, the two-and-a-half grand job?

Again, he was caught in the act.

'Hey, man, I've got the perfect fix on a cool-looking grebe on the far pond. You wanna come and take a look in my viewer?'

'No, I'm good,' he said, far too quickly. After a pause, far too long a pause, he added, 'But thanks for the offer. It looks like a great crested to me. Good spot!' Insult to injury, it sounded like a hollow afterthought, serving only to reinforce the blunt rejection. The silence that followed was as thick as a slab of cold custard, so thick you could cut it with a knife.

Elspeth would have handled it differently. Something along the lines of, 'Oh, I don't want to run the risk of my creaky old knees startling the whole pond.' OK, she had the knack of annoying the hell out of him with her pro-Brexit, anti-vax bollocks, but he would have given the world to see her walk through that door right now.

Elspeth…

***

The phone call had come out of the blue. Clive was away at a conference, she said. She'd got tickets for a film at The Maltings in Wells, she said. OK, he said.

He liked going there, mainly for the classical. They were running a season of old black-and-white films, from the '50s and '60s. Maybe she'd bought seats for the *Birdman of Alcatraz* on account of their shared interest? A tenuous link, it had to be said, but he was looking forward to going. It was always Elspeth and Clive at the quiz night, Elspeth and Clive for lunch at The Pheasant, Elspeth and Clive round for supper and canasta. It would be nice to see her on her own.

He had a vague recollection of seeing the film before, when he was much younger. He couldn't be sure, so he googled it:

A surly convicted murderer held in permanent isolation redeems himself when he becomes a renowned bird expert.

Robert Stroud. American. A convict. A paradox of a man.

During the 43 years he spent in solitary confinement, they have not been able to break him. To this day, he remains unbeaten, unbowed.

They call him The Birdman, and he is the most defiant man alive.

He then watched a three-minute trailer on YouTube. For anyone else it would have been a spoiler, but for him the necessary prelude, the nibble to whet the appetite, the soft whisper of foreplay. Henry Palmer was not one for surprises. Little did he know that he was in for the surprise of his life.

She was already waiting for him in the bar, sipping a G & T.

'Got you an Irish. Jameson's was all they had.'

'Jameson's is fine, thank you. Hello.'

'Hello...' she smiled. 'It's your sixtieth today, isn't it?'

'Yes. But how did you know?'

'Never you mind. Happy birthday, Henry,' she said, leaning forward to give him the lightest of pecks on the cheek.

After the film, most of the crowd headed the few yards down to the quayside to catch the last rays of the sun setting over the creek. Instead, Elspeth grabbed his arm and set off up Staithe Street.

'Come on,' she said, taking his arm.

Where were they going? When she said come, you obeyed. She strode on, head down, as if on a mission.

Crossing the Cromer Road, there was only one place left – The Buttlands. If he were ever to buy a property in Wells-next-the-Sea, it would be here: elegant Georgian square, classic period properties with high-ceilinged rooms, double bay windows and a cellar for the wine. Only last month he'd acted on behalf of a young professional couple who'd bought number 29 in a bidding war. From London, of course. Second home, of course.

She unlinked arms and sped on ahead, straight past the chattering outside tables of The Globe, before disappearing through the front door of The Crown Hotel. Good choice, he remembered thinking. Many a long lunch had been spent there with clients in the front bar. But she wasn't in the bar. He found her sitting in one of the leather chairs at the far end of the reception, flicking through a copy of Country Life. Before he had time to open his mouth, the come-with-me happened again, this time non-verbal. Were her cheeks flushed? He obeyed.

Up the narrow stairs, all the way to the top floor and room 17. She fumbled at the lock.

'Jesus fucking Christ!' she hissed as it blinked red at her.

'Here, let me.' Taking the key card, he turned her red to green.

Flat-screen TV, two distressed leather armchairs, Farrow & Ball maritime paint shades, red and green-checked cushions, tea and coffee tray and a bowl of fruit. In the time it had taken him to scan the room, she had stripped off and was now lying on the double bed on her back, totally naked, save her Chelsea boots.

She had kept her boots on?

Pillow over her face.

Pillow over her face?

Part of him was relieved that she didn't have to see him undress and fumble with the condom she'd left on the bedside table. Part of him wondered whether he was about to audition as her fantasy Burt Lancaster. He'd been listening to the husky tones for an hour and a half, but could he carry the accent off? He could count on the fingers of one hand the number of women he'd slept with, something which he frequently did, just to convince himself that they weren't a figment of his imagination. All of those encounters were about to pale into insignificance…

His first caress drew a muffled cry from beneath the pillow. 'Mew, mew, mew…' sounding for all the world like a circling buzzard calling to its mate.

Her first orgasm began slowly with a hoarse, throaty *ku-ku-cew*, building to an ecstatic bubbling trill before finishing with a loud, 'Hoy! Waup!' Unmistakably curlew. Remarkable!

'Don't stop!' came the muffled command.

She came quickly for a second time with the loud, nasal wailing of an Arctic skua. '*Ahh-yiow, ka-wowee! Ka-wow!*' Extraordinary. He now knew the need for the pillow.

'Again,' she urged.

Orgasmo numero tre was even more aggressive, the deep barking of a great black-backed gull. '*Growk! Ow-ow-ow!*'

'More,' she moaned.

Elspeth saved her best till last, the deep, rhythmic boom of the bittern. '*Ker-wump!* **Ker-whump!**'

Unable to hold back any longer, he joined her with a guttural cry of his own.

Still and sated, pillow now removed, they lay in each other's arms, listening to the distant squabble of seagulls.

She finally broke the silence. 'What was that weird noise you were making when you ejaculated?'

He thought better than to comment on her own climactic crescendos. 'Did I make a noise? Sorry...'

'Actually,' she nuzzled into his chest. 'that was a passably presentable shag, Henry.'

'Well, thank you, Elspeth.'

'The bird call.'

'Yes, of course...'

***

'Excuse me...'

'Oh, er, sorry. I was miles away.'

The man from Des Moines had left his seat to stand in the middle of the hide, a roll-up poised to place between his lips. Piercing blue eyes stared from a pale, stubbled face.

'Bucket list, I said.'

'I beg your pardon?'

'What would your bucket list bird be? What's the one bird you'd love to see on this pond, here, right in front of you, before you died?'

'Er. I'm not sure…'

'I'm going out for a smoke,' he said, placing the cigarette in the corner of his mouth without releasing the stare. You have five minutes.' The door closed behind him with a heavy click.

He sat staring at the back of his hand, doing all he could to stop the trembling, the American's last words playing over and over in his head. *You have five minutes.* He looked at his watch. Four and a half minutes. A highly improbable whirlpool of paranoia was sucking him down.

Killer convict at large. Clive and Elspeth's car in car park. No sign of Clive or Elspeth – hide closed to public. Suspicious American sits where Clive normally sits clad in gear looking like Clive's. Could their bodies be lying there, over the other side of the scrape?

This was stupid. How many people would know Des Moines was the state capital of Iowa? And there probably *was* a nesting pair in the hide. Happened all the time. No, he was imagining things. Three minutes. So what would his bucket list bird be? Bird of paradise? Short-tailed albatross? How incredible would it be to see one of those wheeling in over the marshes to make a splash landing on the scrape?

Try as he might, he couldn't let it go. The face. So pale. A prison pallor. The light blue eyes. Something gnawing deep inside him told him he had seen that face before. The slug of Grey Goose sluiced its way back up into his throat.

'Godber!' he choked. Graham Godber! The case had gripped the nation, back in the 80s when he was at law school. Godber – The Dog Killer.

Seven pensioners he'd killed in all, along with their dogs. Same modus operandi in each case. Frail old souls with frail old pets, mostly rescues, were his carefully selected victims. Stalked their daily routines – where they took their dog for a walk, when they went out shopping, who came to visit. Watched them as they struggled to their local store – one on a Zimmer frame – broke into their homes and gave the dogs a last supper of prime fillet steak before injecting them, tails still wagging, with a lethal dose of pentobarbital. Then hid behind a door or curtain. And waited…

Observed the owner's tortuous return – the fumble at the lock, the shuffling over the threshold, the muttered groan at the ever-present arthritic pain. And then they would see the lifeless form of their poor pet, often the only thing left in their lives, lying on the kitchen floor in a pool of urine. They would cry out its name, drop the shopping bag, limp over to the body and fall to their knees and try to rouse it, sobbing its name over and over again.

And that was when Godber would emerge from his hiding place, creep up behind and slit their throats. Not content with just murdering them, he wanted to witness their anguish. He played with them. Just like he was playing with him now…

Another glance at the watch told him time was up. As if on cue, the door handle lowered with a creak. It was only the slightest of sounds, yet enough to put the whole of the pond to noisy flight. All except one. Unmoved by the collective cry of alarm, the avocet froze mid stride to stare in his direction. Last one standing.

You are my bucket list bird. How could I have possibly thought otherwise? If you are the last living creature I see before I die, then I have lived well.

'I am sorry, my beauty,' he murmured, 'but I am going to

have to disturb you.'

Fight or flight did not even enter his mind as he slowly eased himself up to his feet. Out through the viewing window, then a drop of about six feet and he would be out on the open marsh. At least he would have a chance.

From outside came the sound of a scuffle, ending with the stifled cry of a man. Then the thump of a body hitting the boardwalk, followed by the gasping gurgle of a slashed trachea.

Clive?

Silence.

From under the door, a slow-motion flood of black red blood trickled across the chicken wire floor towards him.

Halfway through the window, he froze.

Glint of sunlight on glass

From across the scrape, in the closed hide.

Someone was watching him.

Still straddling the sill, he raised the Xenon to his eyes.

He let out a gasp

Staring straight back at him, through a pair of binoculars,

Was a fox red Labrador...

SEE EMILY PLAY

'*H*as your mother said anything yet?*'
'About your pile of shit on her lawn? No, she hasn't.'
'I do hope she is impressed.'
Without answering, she quickens her step.

'I hope she is able to appreciate how effectively I modified my diet and movements to achieve optimum issue. Dried figs, mung beans, coal kale. The kale stalks in particular provide the perfect roughage foundation.'

'Please spare me the detail. I really don't want to know.'

He ambushes her just as she is entering The Street, the tempting aroma of charring carcass wafting to her nostrils. He ambushes her just as she is deciding which food stall she is going to choose for breakfast. He ambushes her just as her salivary juices are beginning to flow.

'I do hope she likes it. She will probably have seen it by now. I wanted it to be the first thing your mother saw when she opened the curtains.'

'Well, you will certainly have succeeded in that.' Right in the middle of the lawn. He could have squatted at the far end of the herbaceous border, in amongst the azaleas. Or, even better, behind the gazebo. But no. He dropped his stack bang smack where everyone could see it, in full view of neighbours, passers-by, and visitors to the residence. And that was exactly what he wanted.

'*Do you think she will admire the sweetcorn? I ate twenty cobs yesterday, just to add that special yellow speckle effect.*'

'*You really shouldn't have made the effort.*' Although, by the size of the pile, it must have been quite some remarkable effort, she has to admit to herself. '*I've got to go now, or I'll be late for work.*' Without waiting for an answer, she quickens her pace again and leaves him in her wake. Pushing her way through the rush hour throng, she presses on, trying to fight back the tears. She is angry. Worse than that, she is hungry…

She always wakes up hungry, unable to function without something in her stomach. First thing after teeth, a furtive foray into the chiller room, being careful with the door so as not to rouse the household. A leftover from the previous night's meal – charky buffalo loin, curried yamchops, chipoxli tuna. Better cold, six days old, was what her nana used to say, dog bless her bones.

Having made sure he isn't following her, she doubles back against the complaining commuter stream to plough her way to Willy's Wildkill. Normally a careful eater, she demolishes a double rack of ribs, letting the sticky quokka sauce dribble down her chin.

In other societies, the handsome prince would kneel before his beloved to propose marriage. Not here. Not on Cinnabar. One steaming deposit was all it took to set the train in motion. Some fuckn courtship! The *First Expression of Night Soil* had been made. *On the third presentation of the stool, the host shall give the hand of her daughter to the suitor.* In other words, three strikes and she was out.

Or, to put it more bluntly, three shits and she was out…

Feeling better with food on board, she elbows her way back into the stream. Bit by bit her breathing returns to normal as she allows herself to go with the flow of the morning tide carrying her to the shuttle terminus. There, she descends, traverses, and descends once more to arrive at Gate 9.

She senses the presence of one behind – far too close behind. She catches the scent of his ungenerous urge to squeeze through the barrier before her. That was not going to happen.

The feint of acceleration followed by the abrupt foot plant sends him crashing into her braced back. Oof! He is bigger than she reckoned, but not big enough. She turns on him with a snarl. He snarls back, then retreats with a snort. She nods, apology accepted. As slowly as she can, without walking backwards, she saunters through the gate onto the teeming platform, just in time to board the monorail.

The verdant splendour of the city centre is now left far behind, the austere reality of the industrial outland beckons. Scarred tracts of factories, bridges, and cranes swoosh past, once inaccessible terrains dismantled and transformed into a sprawling landscape of production.

The shuttle slows to walking pace, inviting a guilty peep show into the world of those unfortunate enough to inhabit the terraces below. Staring down wide-eyed into an untidy yard, where a broken swing hangs by a single chain, the harshness of her reality hits home. A single tear runs down her cheek to plop on the floor between her feet.

As the last passenger left in the carriage, she is sorely tempted to stay seated and be carried back to the city. She might as well clock in for another day. What else was there to do? What was there to go back to but an expression of night soil on the lawn, probably still steaming in the morning sun?

***

She trundles, with heavy step, off the platform to join the end of the factory queue. The rust ochre structure looms above them, dwarfing the terminus. All its external trappings – faux oboe strains and fake jojinqua blossom – fail to camouflage the fact that it is a shed. Granted, a big fuckn shed, but a shed nonetheless.

The factory gates open to release the night shift. First out is a young male, sprinting full pelt as if running for his life. He does this every day. And every day she tries to catch a clue from his expression as he races past. Is there a young female somewhere he is desperate to get back to? Is he going to watch a game with the boys? Is he moonshining, maybe? Or is it just that he is so happy to get out? Every day she asks herself the same questions. And every day, she comes up with the same answer. He is just so happy to get out...

Once inside, the autopilot routines kick in – clock on, clean up, struggle into scrubs. She avoids the locker room exchanges like she avoids the disgusting acts of sex they describe in their smutty, cheap chat. Instead, she studies the statement from management pinned to the noticeboard, clearly in response to yesterday's union meeting, where they'd unanimously rejected company claims that conditions were improving and attrition rates falling.

We believe in fair compensation, a safe and healthy working environment, and in providing our workers with a "voice".

Bullshit! They'd had to hold the meeting in secret at the far end of the yards for fear of repercussions. But they'd obviously found out anyway. It went on…

We have the highest entry-level pay of chicken factory communities, we provide excellent dental benefits, and we allow our workers to leave the line to use the lavabo. As final proof of our status as a well-being employer, we can point to a drop of 0.75% in employee self-deaths in the Third Moon, down from 18.5% to 17.75%.

Which was quite good, actually.

The special meeting had been called at short notice and the convenor raced through the formal agenda without interruption. She then signalled the scribe to place her stylus on the table, before proceeding to any other business. Amid much clenching of fists, gnashing of teeth, and animated gesticulation, a heated debate ensued on the issue on everyone's minds – the new line supervisor…

Chicken work was exacting enough, without some new prick on the block trying to make a name for himself. He made the big mistake, as in *big* mistake, of notching up the speed on her line on his very first shift, just a touch; approximately zero point one eight units per cycle. Figured she wouldn't notice.

He figured wrong.

An hour or so in, she steps back from her rig to stretch her shoulders, taut from repetition. For some reason she couldn't quite fathom, the feathers are being particularly tricky today.

A cloud of rancid breathstink signals his arrival. He'd be needing those excellent dental benefits sooner rather than later. Maybe that was why he had joined in the first place? She continues her exercises, forcing him to sidle into her field of vision. He is sporting a thick-rimmed pair of spectacles, an overall in resplendent company colours – brown – and carrying the tools of his supervisory trade. She ignores his name badge. She already has one for him – Clipboard Diq.

'This is a workstation, not a fitness studio,' he sneers.

'Why did the chicken cross the road?' she smiles back.

He jumps into the trap feet first. *'I don't know. Why did the chicken cross the road?'*

'To get away from your stench. Now be a good boy and fuck off. Please leave me alone or I'll knock those stained tombstones down the back of your throat.'

He takes a step back. *'Don't I know you from somewhere?'*

'I sincerely hope not. Now fuck off and let me get on with my work.'

With a parting shot of, *'You shall pay for this, I shall be scrutinising your output,'* he retreats.

The rest of the shift passes without further event. Chicken, chicken, chicken… Try as she might to jettison the thought, a nagging doubt dogs the rest of her morning. Did he know her from somewhere?

They called it *The Beakery,* a dismal attempt to drag the words beak and bakery kicking and screaming into a pathetic pun. Above the servery hatch, gigantic graphics of baguettes, cinnamon swirls and croissants sought to distract from what was actually being baked in the kitchens behind.

The staff canteen – noticeable by its absence from management's roll call of company benefits. Fuckn Beakery. Should have called it *The Giblets*…

When it comes to her turn, she gives the slightest of nods towards the lunchtime special. She'd had enough communication for one day. For communication, read confrontation. You can't have one without the other, it seems. Like love and marriage.

Tray in hand, she retreats to the far corner of the canteen to a table fronded by the ferns of a synthetic quaxl oak. With no regard for dignity, she plonks herself down on the bench with such force that a couple of replica acorns eject from the tree's canopy to bounce, then roll, across the floor until coming to rest under the table of two young females. They look up from their lunch then quickly down again, both possessing sufficient emotional intelligence and survival instinct to know better than to ask whether she is going to pick them up. The triple T-bone combo is wolfed down without ceremony, followed by a palate-cleansing wild squirrel sorbet, followed by a squeaky fart.

Then, across the crowded room, she sees him. Weaving his way in slow motion between the tables towards her, balancing his tray on an upturned palm like a high-class waiter, she is relieved that she got the fart out of the way.

It is Tupoc – younger than her by a good few years, but sharp as a blade. Of the hundred or so workers occupying the canteen, he alone looked wowsers in the company scrubs. The raise of an eyebrow seeks permission to join her. She nods, then smiles. He is worth more than a nod. So much more…

He smiles back as he slides in beside her. '*So, how's it going?*'

'*Bad as bad can be.*'

Leaving the tray untouched, he looks askance at her. She is not one to let the world get to her.

'*How so?*'

'*Best you eat your food first, then I'll tell.*' Just to get the ball rolling, she reaches across to snaffle a rib from his plate. '*Mmm, quite passable, for once.*'

'*Good to hear. I'm sure I would have enjoyed it.*' He takes a rib from his plate while there are still some left. They eat in studied concentration. *'So, do you want to tell me what's up? It's the new line supervisor, isn't it?'*

'No, it's not him, the weedy little wankpipe. I can deal with him. And I will deal with him.'

The two young females look across at her. Maybe she'd communicated that a little too loudly. She stares back and they look away, feigning deep conversation.

'So what's the problem?'

'It's Xilox. Expression of Night Soil.'

'What! For you?'

'Yes. No need to sound so surprised.'

'No, er, I didn't mean… Where?'

'On Mother's lawn.'

'Oh my. On your mother's lawn. That takes some balls.'

There is a pause as she works her way through a mouthful of mango, again from his plate. She swallows.

'He even shat sweetcorn so that it was in a pattern.'

'Wow! What sort of pattern?'

'Triangles – speckly, yellow triangles.'

'Equilateral?'

'Yes, I think – listen, who gives a fuck what sort of triangles! Do you want me to get him to send you over a set of design drafts?'

'No, er, sorry, I'd better go. You be at Crumple tonight?'

'Maybe,' she shrugs.

'See you there, then. If you do go, that is.' He stands, shifting from foot to foot.

'I thought you were going, Tupoc.' She swaps plates and hoovers his clean. When she looks up, he is gone. She plays his words over in her head. *That takes some balls.* And he was

right. Not every young male would dare to do what Xilox did. And if Tupoc had been impressed, Mother was sure to be. She didn't take shit from anybody...

***

To her six girls, she was just Mother. To the rest of the world, Ophelia Weintraub was a formidable female to be respected, revered, or feared, depending on where and how your paths crossed. Her position of privilege had spared her from the excesses of Diktat 7. In recognition of her stature in society, she had been permitted to retain her residence with its stunning Italianate gardens, their perfectly clipped topiaries and manicured lawns sweeping down to the boulevard. She reminded herself every day that she could lose it all in a heartbeat.

Above her desk, the study wall is covered with citations, certificates and diplomas as visual symbols of a long and distinguished career, each framed in the sought-after black ebony of the rift valley forest, each a tribute to her devout servitude to Dog. Six gold cups stand on the mantelpiece, testament to her prowess with the rod, pride of place going to the World Series Trophy, now in her permanent possession after six successive defences.

The memory brings a smile to her lips. Throughout the day, the crowds had gathered to witness her titanic struggle with the serpent. Throughout the night, the dwellers of that far-flung isle on the brink of the western sphere feasted on the purple flesh of the beast. She could still hear their songs of celebration in the village square. She could still taste the liquorice-salty tang of the meat. She could still feel the burn of the quinquixa shots on the back of her throat…

***

The dog comes through the wall and helps itself to a Havana from the black cedar cigar box on the coffee table.

Ophelia jumps up from her desk with a start. *'My Lord, you arrive unannounced. Had I known, I would have prepared for you a bowl of treats.'*

'The cigar is fine,' it replies. *'Please join me.'*

She obeys, respectfully waiting for her guest to bloss first. She finally raises her eyes.

'To what do I owe this honour, My Lord? And why…' She stops herself.

'Pray continue…'

'And why, if I may make so bold as to ask, why the unconventional entrance?'

'Dog moves in a mysterious way.'

She bows her head. *'Of course, My Lord.'* She has been a fool to question. She has gone too far.

The dog stubs out the cigar in the quartz crystal ashtray. *'I am here to speak about your daughter…'*

Her heart sinks. All her girls had fled the nest to forge paths of their own. Stellar careers, steady partners, intelligent offspring. All except one. Emily…

Before she can express remorse, pray for forgiveness, the dog continues.

'You must be aware that Xilox has deposited an Expression of Night Soil in her name.'

She nods.

'*He is a fine young male of good standing. I ask you a simple question, Ophelia Weintraub. Is she worthy of him?*'

It is all she can do to suppress her shock and anger. That her inventive, witty, talented daughter should not be worthy of that dull, humourless, mind-numbingly boring mogg of a male? It was a match made in the stars.

The dog is, of course, able to read her every thought at such close quarters.

'*You are ignoring to take into account her deviant tendencies, Ophelia.*'

'*You speak of her transgression at the bibliotek, My Lord?*'

'*Transgressions – plural. Six counts of unauthorised research.*'

'*She has repented her sins, My Lord. And she has accepted the sanction. For three moons now, she has worked at the chicken factory without missing a single shift, even though such travail is beneath her station.*'

A snarl. '*Surely I need not remind you, Ophelia Weintraub, how critical such work is to our mission?*'

'*Forgive me, My Lord.*' She averts her gaze, mortified that she allowed herself to venture out onto thin ice again. One more slip like that and the Italianate garden would be nothing but a distant memory, a sickening crunch of cypress branch in the recycling crusher.

The dog takes a second cigar, lights it, and blows a thick billow out into the room. This time, there is no invitation for her to join it. The bloss of smoke forms a ring of rabbits, circling and circling until they disperse.

'*Are you aware that she frequents the place they call The Crumple Zone?*'

Her jaw drops.

'Your reaction tells me not so.'

'I beg for forgiveness, My Lord,' she winces. *'I shall forbid her from ever setting foot in the place again.'*

'That will not be necessary. In fact, you must not mention it at all. It serves a purpose for us to know that all the dissidents and deviants are gathered in one place. We have them where we want them.'

'But, My Lord...'

'Technically speaking, she is not breaking her sentence conditions by going there. But if, in doing so, she violates Diktat 7, then I do not need to remind you of the consequences.'

'No, My Lord.'

'Good. Thank you for the cigars, Ophelia. Excellent, as always.'

'The honour and pleasure are entirely mine, My Lord.' She watches the dog melts through the wall, pads across the lawn and circles the faecal edifice deposited by Xilox, sniffing as it goes. After what seems a lifetime, it finally cocks its leg.

The piss is passed. The die is cast. There shall be a wedding. Ophelia breathes a deep sigh of relief, reaches with trembling hand for the cut-glass decanter on the drinks tray, and pours herself a stiff fandango.

***

Saying no to the needle with a quick shake of her head, Emily Weintraub barrels into the tattoo parlour. She weaves her way through the yelping clients to the door that says staff only. Once inside, she heads across the restroom to the unmarked portal behind the pinball machine. Her fingers tap softly on the door – this week's password is the opening three bars of

'Yellow Submarine'. The hatch slides open to reveal two jade eye slits through the grille. A single blink, the draw of a bolt, and the door opens just enough to allow her to sidle in – the classic speakeasy.

Except that nobody spoke easy any more. In fact, nobody spoke at all...

Without so much as a glance at the duty muscle, she strides purposefully down the corridor, pausing only to take in the cartoon strip tapestry running its length. The owner of the joint – rich and anonymous – had commissioned the piece from the loomster co-operative down on the Old Docks. A remarkable work, it depicted in intricate and graphic detail what Wilma and Betty got up to when Fred and Barney went bowling. Fellatio, cunnilingus, and – dare she even let the thought enter her head – doggy style. What a multitalented, versatile, and very naughty boy that Dino was. All very explicit. And all very much in defiance of Diktat 7.

Never one for the quiet entrance, she brushes through the chain-link curtain, turning the heads of the occupants of nearby tables; heads that turn back quickly on realisation of who it is. On bar duty is Stog, fully plated. Things could get kinda playful in the early hours at The Crumple.

'*What's it to be?*'

'*What's on happy hour tonight?*'

'*Whisky sour, screwdriver, and Sex in an Elevator.*'

'*I'll take all three. In a highball.*'

He grimaces. '*Really? Been that kinda day, huh?*'

'*Yup,*' she nods.

'*OK, as you wish. The customer is always right.*' He turns his back to mix her drink, shaking his head. He gives her a half glance over his shoulder. '*The customer is also barred if she kicks off like she did the last time she ordered a whisky sour, screwdriver and Sex in an Elevator,'* he grunts.

'*Understood,*' she sighs.

Of course he knows about the night soil on her mother's lawn. But, like any good barman, he probes no further, serves her drink, takes her copper zecs, and returns to wiping glasses with the dirty cloth tucked into his waistband.

She takes the table at the very far end of the stage, from where she has an unrestricted view of the cavern. Directly opposite, reedy strains of Miles Davis drift from the Blue Room, where cool, young couples groove to the vibe. Adjacent, the black hole of the Peyote Pit; where souls and minds turn inside out.

And then, the stage, the expanse of board on which songs were once sung, plays once played, comedies once capered. My, how gloriously uplifting that must have been. Entertaining and often thrillingly inventive though it often was, today's meagre menu of music and dance, mime and circus seems paltry fare compared to those feasts of the past. There are only so many times you can give a standing ovation to six acrobats standing on each other's shoulders. Mind you, she has to remind herself that she always does enjoy the finale, where Stog steps out from behind the bar, buckles a juvenile to the wheel, sets it spinning and hurls the axes.

She takes a mouthful of the bittersweet cocktail and holds it there, allowing the silent buzz of conversation to seep into her senses. The main floor is beginning to fill up with couples and after-work cliques, pretending to be in social mode but still on guard.

Thankfully, no one from the chicken factory is there. The table gives her a perfect view of the door and enough time to shift to somewhere more discreet should any of her line colleagues show up. There was, of course, one exception, one figure she would dearly love to see emerge through those chains. She was the one who'd said maybe. And now her heart aches for that maybe to materialise.

She knows he won't show. Story of her life – maybes remaining maybes.

Certainly, in his case, nothing could be counted on. Whenever she tried to ask him about his life – where he lived, his family, the special flexible working arrangements he had at the factory – he clammed up. He was definitely hiding something. He was... what's the word...? Cagey.

Cagey, that's what he was.

Cagey...

***

There are hangovers and then there are hangovers.

In hindsight, it was a big, big mistake to seek solace in the Peyote Pit. Just one blow. Just one, she'd promised to herself. That's what they all say. All she'd wanted to do was have some fun, shine like the sun, drift away on a misty lullaby. Instead, she went to a party down a red dirt road, where she did some Cinnabar dust with a blind rogue dog. It took her by the hand and guided her through a shapeshift until they sat round a campfire singing stupid songs with a pack of freaked out saplings.

Then today of all days, Clipboard Diq is waiting at her station to tell her she is being transferred over to Navigation. He looks none too pleased. Normally, this would have been music to her ears, an escape from the mindless repetition of the production line, but how was she going to concentrate with a serious case of the judders?

They give her a Rhode Island Red for its final fit; a handsome bird with lustrous deep pink plumage and black tail, its single comb, earlobes and wattle a vivid red. She manages the wiring OK, but inserting the Cinnabar solution into the tiny fuel tank proves more of a challenge. Twice she has to step back to wipe her magnifying glass clean, unclog her pipette, unclog her mind. Finally, she is ready to submit her cluckbot for inspection. A serious-looking scrutineer called Katarina gives it the thumbs up and she gently places it on the departure belt.

'Dog speed, little one,' she smiles.

From her seat beneath the quaxl oak, her plate barely touched, she sees him weave his way toward her. Boy, would she give him a piece of her mind.

'So, where were you last night?' he frowns.

'Where was I? Fuckn cheek! I might ask you the same question.'

'At our usual table. Sat waiting for you. All night.'

Crap, he must have arrived when she was in the Peyote Pit. She doesn't want him to know she was in there.

'Oh, I... er, must have missed you when I slipped into the Blue Room for a chill.'

A slight tilt of the head to one side tells her he is not convinced. But he moves on.

'Such a shame you missed the big news.'

'Big news? What big news?'

'The announcement.'

'Don't mess with me, Tupoc. What announcement?'

'It took us all by surprise. Stog stepped out from behind the bar, went up onto the stage, unfurled a banner and pinned it to the back wall.'

'And?'

'To mark a year of staying open, next moon's talent comp is going to have the biggest ever jackpot. Seven trillion...'

Emily Weintraub's eyebrows attempt orbit. Seven trillion! She jumps up from her seat.

'Where are you going? Aren't you going to finish your food?'

'I've got to make a call...'

***

The ball court is deserted at this early hour, a good place to gather your thoughts, rehearse your lines. Only last moon, she was playing here to a packed house, not a space to be found on the banks of stone seats flanking the playing area. Of course, Mother disapproved. Pok-ta-pok was no kind of activity a daughter of hers should be engaged in. Instinctively, she runs her fingers along her hips, elbows, and knees, the only parts of the body allowed to hit the hard rubber ball. In spite of the heavy padding and belt – part protective, part ceremonial – the bruising goes deep and is still tender to the touch.

What a game that was! She chuckles to herself as she recalls how she'd taken out their guard with a monster hit on the first play, before slotting the ball through the sunrise ring with ease. The crowd went wild.

'Tank! Tank! Tank!' they screamed.

After a fight fought hard, victory was theirs. In former times, the losers would be sacrificed, their honour in shreds.

Nowadays, they just had to kneel centre court and eat the red dust.

But now all is still, quiet as the grave. The Tank looks up at the empty terraces, suddenly feeling very alone, vulnerable. Taking a deep breath, she trundles off the court, out into the main ceremonial plaza, where gigantic, truncated pyramids stand guard on either side. Watching her. Waiting for her next move...

She sets off at pace, head down to avoid any risk of chance encounter. Only when she enters the Place of Shadow does she finally summon up the courage to raise her eyes. She lets out a gasp. Towering ten score times her height over her, the terrifying manifestation of power and knowledge, is the colossal jade statue of the almighty dog-god. Here she sits, visible from every part of the city, her gleaming red good eye reading their movements, the black hole of her gouged eye reading their minds.

God of fire and lightning
God of monsters
God of deformity
The dog-god Xolotl...

Of course, she has been here before, as one of the congregated mass, head bowed, to mark Fifth Sun renewal. But she's never been here alone, and she is wondering what the fuck made her decide to choose this of all places. The unblinking stare from the red eye issues a fierce command to kneel and she obeys at once.

Eyes tightly closed, she autopilots into the 'Exodus Canticle'.

'Blessed are you, Dog of our ancestors,
Worthy to be praised and exalted forever.

You have delivered us from the dominion of darkness.
'Cross firmaments to our promised land.

You have raised up a mighty salvation for us
In your holy dwelling, the planet of the dog.

Blessed are you, Dog of our ancestors,
Worthy to be praised and exalted forever.

Let us rejoice with you, O Dog,
In the bountiful harvest of the Sacred Dust!

When you send forth your spirit, all is made good.
You renew the face of the earth.

Blessed are you, Dog of our ancestors,
Worthy to be praised and exalted forever.

Set a watch before my mouth, O Dog,
And guard the door of my lips.

You have shown strength with your arm,
To punish those who cause your heart to harden.

Blessed are you, Dog of our ancestors,
Worthy to be praised and exalted forever...'

The red eye releases its grip but she remains kneeling, breathing in and out, deep and slow, to try to get her heart rate back to normal. She scratches at her left hand, a painful reminder of what happens when Dog's heart is hardened. In addition to the ritual, postnatal removal of a digit, a second had been severed as punishment for the bibliotek episode. Three members of her vicious dog squad had burst into her cell in the middle of the night, stuck a numbshot into her arm, and gone to work with the saw. The ghost appendage still aches of a cold morning.

The faintest of tremors announces the arrival of another. She knows it to be Xilox. *The fool would do anything I say*, she smiles.

'*Good day,*' she twitches.

'*Good day. How fitting. I assume you have called me here to discuss our marriage plans, here in the presence of Dog – order of service, guest list, honeymoon. I am sure we shall receive her blessing.*'

'*Let us not get ahead of ourselves, Xilox.*'

'*How so, dearest? My second expression is surely the strongest testimony of my feelings for you.*'

'*Second expression?*' Oh for fuck's sake, he's only gone and crapped on the lawn again!

'*I sense you have not yet seen my latest creation? Eggplant spirals studded with pomegranate seeds...*'

'*Stop there, Xilox!*'

'*I do not understand your reluctance to...*'

'*It's a pile of steaming shit, Xilox.*'

'*No, you are so wrong. It is so much more than that. It is proof of the esteem I hold for your family, proof of the respect I hold for you.*'

'*Esteem. Respect. What about love?*'

'*What's love got to do...?*'

'*Got to do with it? Everything, Xilox. Everything...*'

Their thought waves founder slowly onto the shingly sand of a barren beach. Time for her to ride the big roller.

'*I have a proposal for you.*'

'*But... I do not understand. I am the one proposing.*'

'*My proposal is of a different nature. You withdraw your offer of betrothal...*'

'*But Emily!*'

'*Listen! You withdraw your pledge, and I will pay you five trillion zecs.*'

He does not respond. That is good. He is thinking about it.

Finally, he lets out a deep sigh. '*But how would I begin to explain to my family, to our friends? To your mother?*'

'*If you can manage to express eggplant spirals studded with pomegranate seeds, Xilox, I'm sure you can find a way. Do we have a deal?*'

He stares into the distance. '*Will you let me still be in your axe-throwing team?*'

So sweet. So sad. '*OK, all right then.*'

He turns away. '*We have a deal.*'

***

To join her on the big night, she has chosen her two favourite childhood dolls, a toy dinosaur named Dino – what else? – and an old Italian sailor called Enzo. Stone certain, she could not rehearse in Mother's house – a secret at home is like rocks under tide, as the saying goes. So, she smuggles her two dolls to her works locker which she reinforces with a Klampit. A destitute container, at the far end of a forgotten fork of the marshalling yards, is where she takes them between night shifts. Inside, she has fitted out the far end with a floor-to-ceiling, wall-to-wall mirror, illuminated by 17 j teuton bulbs. And there, night after night, perched on a stool, a doll on each knee, she rehearses.

Slight smile, lips parted. Teeth lightly touching, just enough to allow the tongue to move. And then, contract the diaphragm, keep the airway constricted so that breath is trapped in the throat, exhale slowly and… speak.

It is as if her whole life has been waiting for this moment. *Is there no play to ease the anguish of a torturing hour?* Oh, how she had loved Shakespeare. Untimely ripped from their parlours, book clubs, and theatres. No more Macbeths, no more Merry Wives of Windsor, no more Merchants of Venice. Stone certain, she could not break Dog's law by speaking anywhere, let alone on a stage. So…

She will speak while not speaking; speak unspeakable speech with closed lips. She will utter unutterable comedy without utterance. She will entertain them. She will liberate them. She will blow their tiny minds with her new interpretation of the ancient art form discovered at the bibliotek when she went off-piste to rifle through those hidden manuscripts in the archive room. Sure, she paid the price. But now it is payback time.

One night, midsession, she takes a break out in the yard to stretch her limbs. Above the dark hulk of the chicken factory, as constellations sparkle their presence. *Twinkle, twinkle little star…* One of her first memories, the tantalising, hypnotic lilt of a nursery rhyme on Mother's lips as she sat on her knee.

Somewhere out there, the tiny rock they call Earth. Home to *Homo sapiens*. The new species on their old planet. A species which inspired the greatest cultural craze of generations, a golden epoch of obsession with the intoxicating, artistic creativity of Man: fashion, music, dance, drama, architecture, and literature. In which their language – sapspeak – became the new vernacular naif, the new primitive cool. Diktat 7 put an end to all that, the Command which outlawed the speaking of sap as a cardinal sin. Almost overnight, society was catapulted back into old-school argots of ancestral communities, hardwired syntax of visual, auditory, and tactile communication with their complex pheromonic amalgams of sense and thought. A world of unspoken understandings. A muzzled world.

So engrossed is she in her musings, that she doesn't sense the presence of another, just out of thought-shot, lurking in the shadows. She is not alone…

***

'*Have you tried these chinchilla sticks? They are terrific!*'

'*Yes, I have. And only last week you said they tasted like a straw suppository.*'

She ignores his truth. '*And they are the perfect accompaniment to the pickled squink, don't you think?*'

He doesn't answer immediately, but stirs his hazy Grenache sundae with a spoon. Then he takes the plunge.

'*Are you on something?*'

'*Hold that thought there uno secondo, I just have to get more of this cool cuisine.*'

The table is almost removed from its moorings as she leaps

up from her seat to send half a dozen acorns bouncing in her wake. Having jumped – as in, half demolished – the queue at the counter, she returns with another plateful.

'*Smask, smask,*' she dribbles, '*this mushbog parfait is astonishing! A furious blizzard of svampoq and ostrom as smooth as premier-grade billiard baize stroked the right way, with just that touch of give. They certainly know how to knock out a good dish here. Seriously biff!*'

The stare from Tupoc is as blank as blank can be. She must be on something. He concentrates on stirring his Grenache, while she licks her lips, daintily wipes the sticky corners of her mouth with a towel, and sits back with the glazed look of a contented female contemplating a fart.

'*So, are you going to tell me what's up?*'

'*How do you mean?*'

'*You know as well as I do, the only reason we come here to eat is that there's nowhere else to go. And the second only reason we come here to eat is to complain about the dog-awful food they serve up.*'

'*Oh, come on Tupoc, it's not that bad...*'

'*And will you wipe that stupid grin off your face, Emily! I really don't like you when you're like this.*'

'*Oh-ho! So do I detect here a corollary, Tupoc, whereby there is an alternate version of Emily that you really do like?*'

The young male leans away from the curveball and returns to stirring his Grenache. If only he could close his eyes and drift away to a lazy sundae in another corner of the canteen.

'*It's just that you're being so bloody... positive, Emily. I'm not used to it, that's all. Don't get me wrong, I understand how tough it is for you right now. All that business with Xilox...*'

'*Oh, did I not tell you about his second expression?*'

'No...'

'Yes, you would be seriously impressed, Tupoc. A perfect pyramid garnished with eggplant spirals.'

'But...'

'Wait, the best is yet to come. Each of the ribbons is studded with pomegranate seeds. The effect is amazing!'

A long communication break follows as he stares over the heads of diners at the Fire Exit sign. He coughs.

'So everything's now OK between you and Xilox, then?'

'No, of course not! Whatever gives you that idea?' she laughs.

'The fact that you appear more than happy with a second deposit on your mother's lawn, that's why!'

She places her hand on his – for the first time. He does not withdraw.

'The appearance of a second expression is immaterial. There will be no wedding, Tupoc,' she smiles.

He blinks rapidly. 'No wedding? I don't understand.'

'Xilox has agreed not to pursue his suit if I pay him five trillion zecs.'

'What?'

'Xilox has agreed not to pursue his suit if I pay him five trillion zecs. Now would you like me to chisel the sentence on your forehead so that you can remember it?'

'But, but, that's a small fortune! Where are you going to get your hands on that kind of money? Surely not from your mother?'

'Of course not, dumbum. No, I'm going to win first prize in The Crumple Zone Talent Contest.'

'You have got to be joking!'

'Do I look like a comedy act?' O ye of little faith, she thinks to him.

Oh shit, he thinks to himself. Oh shit...

***

The Seven Moons of Cinnabar, locked in celestial coupling with their magnetic mother planet, orbit thirteen times above her apricot atmosphere, their lunar paths marking the immutable passage of time. The day of the contest nears...

Each new dawn brings with it a growing sense of destiny. Buoyed by the intelligence squeezed from Stog on the other sixteen acts – her main rival contenders being an elderly couple copulating on a high wire – Emily's confidence climbs. The rest comprises a schmaltzy, uninspiring medley of mime, dance, and bluegrass. Same old sewage they'd been swallowing since Diktat 7. Added to which, the rehearsals in the darkest recesses of the marshalling yards were reaping nightly rewards.

Script – nailed, word perfect.

Doll dialogue – crisp and tight.

Manipulation and expression – almost there. Not easy balancing and working a puppet on each knee, but getting the hang of it.

And, most important of all, how to manage her smile, her eyes, and her expression. The raised eyebrow of disbelief at sailor boy's outrageous assertions, the shared smirk with the audience at Dino doll's responses. To assist, she takes an inhalant of aloe juice to lubricate her postcranial pneumatics.

Hard to admit it, but she gets the competitive thing from Mother. Not for her, though, the reeling in of a monster fish on some dogforsaken strand. Instead, she chooses to cause carnage on the pok-ta-pok court and cry havoc at cheeky choppers on axe-throwing nite. Like a Boudicca on full charge, she feels that her time has come. But she knows this is going to be the toughest play of all...

***

The day arrives.

Awake for most of the night, revisiting the logistics over and over in her head, she is confident that she has all bases covered – the journey to work, getting through the two shifts on Production, smuggling her gear to Crumple, final preps in the dressing room and then, deep breath, out onto the boards.

Cigar smoke seeps from under the study door into the vestibule. Mother must be up early. Keen to bypass the usual car crash of pre-breakfast conversation, Emily pads softly over to the front door and reaches for the handle. There she freezes, heart racing, the tips of her remaining fingers resting on the cool metal.

A bead of sweat rolls down her forehead and drops from the tip of her nose onto the mosaic tiles with a plop. She is unable to press down on the handle, knowing that there was one thing, the only thing, that could still fuck everything up. She snorts twice, opens the door, and steps out into the cool morning air. A panicky scan of the front estate confirms that no third splatch of night soil has been deposited. Xilox has honoured the deal. She is ready to rumble…

Her understated costume of denim tux avec crimson cummerbund lay ready and waiting – washed, ironed, and neatly folded – in her locker. To the outside world, it would be the same old Emily Weintraub, setting off to the chicken plant for another day on the line.

She goes with the flow of the rush-hour tide before drifting cross-current to Willy's Wildkill.

'*Usual?*'

'*Yes, please.*'

A few tables are set back from the street, behind a bamboo screen to shield from traffic dust. She takes the furthest one, out of sight from the main drag. The last thing she wants is a chance encounter with Xilox.

The rack of ribs is reverently consumed right down to the last lick of quokka sauce from the bones. Leaving a top-heavy tip, she waves a goodbye to rejoin the throng, allowing herself to be carried down the street towards the terminus. Down at Gate 9, a beefsteak male attempts a shoulder edge on her. She lets him pass – no distractions today. She steps back to be last on board.

Staring through the window at the ironscape rushing past, she rehearses her lines, jaw clenched in a taut smile. The shuttle slows on cue on the embankment. Her eyes mist over at the sight of a female juvenile on a swing, a mended swing, going so high she almost loops. The child is whooping with joy. It is a sign. That swing was broken for a long, long time.

First out of the carriage, she heads for the queue at the cluckbot shed. When the gates open, she instinctively looks for sprinting boy. He is not there. Then she spots him, amongst the last to leave, arm in arm with the pretty little thing who massacres the sausage hash at the Beakery. Avoiding all contact, she clocks in and moves through to Transition, where she goes to her locker, undoes the padlock, checks for her holdall hidden under the bottom shelf, and changes into her scrubs.

For some reason, she is back on Operations – chicken feet. She is good with that. Repetition without needing to concentrate is good today. Without realising, she exceeds her quota for the first shift. Thankfully, Clipboard Diq does not pester her once throughout the whole day. Instead, he sticks to patrolling the furthest line, next to the lavabos. Maybe he has tummy troubles, she hopes. At one point, towards the end of the afternoon, she looks up to catch him staring straight at her across the factory floor. Is that a smile on his face?

***

Stog greets her with a startled look.

'*You're early. The show doesn't start for another two hours yet.*'

'*I know,*' she grins. '*Just wanted to lubricate the gills first. Might just dive straight into one of your cocktails. That Sex in an Elevator was good. Actually, it was excellent. Selling well?*'

'*Up and down.*'

'*Oof, that hurt! Pour me one.*'

'*You sure? Not the best idea to get wagtailed if you're going up there,*' he nods towards the stage.

'*Grateful for your concern, but I'm just having the one, just to get in the groove.*'

'*As you wish…*'

The place is pretty full already, mainly with the after-work crowd. Rather than make herself too comfortable, she props herself up against the bar. The first sip of the six-spice spirit causes her nostrils to flare as she holds it in her mouth. She surveys the scene. The tables are pressed in right up to the front of the stage, leaving just enough room for the retro scoreboard listing each of the acts and setting out the rules of the contest. She knows them off by heart.

Each paying punter votes by pressing one of the two buttons on their pinger – green for a like, red for a dislike.

Only ten pings are allowed per act. At the end of the contest, the scores are totted up and the act with the highest number of green minus red pings is the winner. Writ large at the bottom stand the mandatory three 'H's:

NO HECKLING!
NO HOCKLING!
NO HURLING!

She empties her glass, smacks her lips and heads backstage.

The dimly lit corridor with bare zeebloc walls leads her to the brightly lit dressing room with bare zeebloc walls. The decor is spartan and then some, all furniture and fittings free-standing for ease of swift evacuation in the event of a visit from the dog squad. She is first in, as planned, and chooses the locker in the far corner. Before she places her holdall into safekeeping, she unzips it for a final check.

She screams…

***

Tupoc had only just signed in for his shift when the message came, so checking out again so soon without the necessary authorisations had not been easy. She had sounded in a terrible state. *Get here now!* was all she sent, over and over again.

He arrives to find her slumped in the corner of the dressing room, eyes closed, chin resting on knees, four empty bottles around her feet. Most of the other contestants are there, going through their routines. Although there was hardly enough room for them all, they were wise enough to leave a clear quadrant of space in front of the figure in the corner.

He notes the glances darting in her direction, her competitors expecting the figure to burst into life at any moment and launch into her act. What were those bottles for? The smart money was on her making a set of pan pipes with the bottles to summon up a king cobra out of the open bag beside her. How predictable! Absolutely no need to worry about her, then...

His efforts to rouse her fail to raise any response, so he races back to the bar, where he grabs Stog's attention.

'*There are others in front of you.*'

'*I know, but it's her. She needs help.*'

'*Stage fright, huh?*'

'*Worse.*'

Stog pours a pitcher of iced water and plops in a kabba bean.

'*Two!*'

'*Really? That bad? OK, if you say so...*'

Back in the dressing room, he forces her to drink the treacly cocktail. The effect is instantaneous. She opens her eyes, stares at him, then at the open holdall, then back at him. Then she howls.

'*I'm fucked!*'

He places a hand on her shoulder. '*Easy, easy, just try and tell me exactly what's happened.*'

'*Look!*' she points. Inside the bag lay a dino puppet and beside it, a block of wood. '*Some bastard's stolen Enzo!*' she moans.

'*But, but, who would do a thing like that? Xilox?*'

'*No, he'd never do such a thing. And he doesn't know about this, either. I'm fucked...*'

'*But, but, surely you can still go through with it with just the dino?*'

'*Of course I can't!*' she snarls at him, removing his hand from her shoulder. '*The whole act is the dialogue with the sap. I've written the script, rehearsed the lines. It's too late to come up with something new. I am totally fucked!*'

Tupoc scratches his chin. '*You're on last, I think you said?*'

'*Yes.*'

'*So what time would that be?*'

'*Fuck knows.*'

'*I'm trying to help here, Emily. Please try and be more precise.*'

'*Five past fuck knows, then.*'

He scratches his chin again. '*Get your costume on. Rehearse your lines. I will be back.*'

'*But...*'

'*Do as I say, Emily. I will be back, I promise.*' He turns tail and leaves.

Halfway along the corridor, he stops, makes sure no one is looking, then blinks seven times and releases three burps in the key of D minor – his personal neuro-ID. *Please wait while your bank is checking your details.* He's in! A quick scan tells him he is going to need every last zec. He goes out into the crowded cavern, pulls his collar up and slips into the Peyote Pit.

Head down, fingers clasped tightly around the small package in his coat pocket, he heads into the centre, walking as quickly as he dares without attracting unwanted attention. In spite of the chill night wind whipping across the Main Plaza, he is sweating skips. What is he doing?

At daybreak, he recites the Oath religiously with neither fail nor falter. He never crosses a junction on a purple light.

He pays all his taxes on time. Tupoc has never so much as entertained the thought of breaking a law in his whole life, so what he was doing now was utter madness! One false slip and he would be looking at a twenty-year stretch, at the very least – his career, his reputation, his whole life in ruins. No, he was being too hasty; he cannot just rush into this. He needs to think this through...

So he veers sinister and goes to a place where he can regain a sense of composure, the place where he can be at one with himself. To his relief, the ball court is empty. He climbs up the steep steps to the very top of Block H and takes the very last seat in the row, right up against the scoreboard. This is his asylum, a refuge from a world of controlled ritual, his retreat from a society of decreed dogma. She doesn't know it, but this is where he watches her every match day. Some of the best times of his life are spent here, the crowd going crazy as she dumps the opposition star striker on her arse. '*E–mi–ly! E–mi–ly!*'

He stares down at the pitch, flurries of red dust being whipped up by the sharpening wind. He shivers. He hadn't promised her anything, other than that he would return. He had no idea whether he would be able to see his plan through. He had no idea how he would be able to cope with the shame and guilt if he were caught. And he had no idea whether she had the slightest chance of winning the contest, even if she had her two props. This is sheer madness. Tupoc shakes his head, sighs heavily through his nostrils and gets slowly to his feet.

Fuck it. He was going to see Emily play...

He knew the duty guards would be surprised to see him back, but he hadn't expected such a hostile reception.

'*What the hell are you doing here?*' glowers Uriq.

'*You're not supposed to be here,*' hisses Ankl. '*We are putting our necks on the line letting you break your shift in the first place. You know the rules!*'

'*Listen, guys, I'm...*'

'*Family emergency,*' you said. '*Must have been some fuckn emergency for you to be back so soon. What was it this time? Grandad got his dick caught in his zip again? On your way, Tupoc.*'

He pulls the small package from his coat pocket, opens it, and taps its contents out on the countertop, ever so slowly. Ever so quickly, their beady eyes sparkle.

'*Luludust, prime cut,*' Tupoc winks. '*Just by way of appreciation for your... understanding.*'

'*Fine, sure,*' frowns Uriq, not taking his eyes off the purple powder for one moment. Ankl is already out back in the stores searching for a funnel. '*Just don't let it happen again.*'

Without waiting for a reply, Uriq bends down to press the door release button. Without looking back, Tupoc steps through.

Once inside, he leans against the wall and closes his eyes, pressing his back hard against the cold surface to stop his shaking. That was far too close for comfort. He opens his eyes to face the black-and-white images, the grainy, moving footage of the permanent exhibition displayed on the wall opposite. The single act of sacrilege that changed the course of their history, forever etched into the collective conscience of their race.

Laika.

A tear rolls down his cheek. Although time is of the essence, he is forced to read the obituary.

A stray mongrel from the streets of Moscow,
she was selected to be the sole occupant of the Soviet spacecraft,
Sputnik 2,
launched Earth year 1957.
The sap scientists assumed that such animals had already
learned to endure
extremes of cold, hunger, and danger.
Nothing could have prepared the female dog for what she would
face.
To adapt the dog to the confines of the tiny cabin,
she was kept in progressively smaller cages
for periods of up to 20 days.
The extensive close confinement
caused her to stop urinating or defecating,
made her anxious,
caused her condition to deteriorate.
She was placed in a centrifuge
to simulate the acceleration of a rocket launch.
She was placed inside machines
to simulate the deafening noises of a spacecraft.
Harnessed inside the capsule,
she was restricted by chains.
There was no room for her to turn around.
No capacity for her recovery was planned
because her survival was never expected.
The Soviet government claimed that she was euthanised
prior to oxygen depletion.
This was a lie.
Laika died a terrible death of overheating and suffocation
five hours into the flight.

Tupoc sheds a second tear.

Man, you should not have done that.

MAN... you should not have done that!

It didn't have to be like this. Out of ancestral loyalty and love, the dogs had patrolled the planet for centuries, maintaining a light-touch, custodial presence in the form of deities and mythical folklore beasts indulging in the occasional act of carnage – Cerberus, Fenrir, The Beast of Flanders, Black Shuck... But that all changed overnight, thanks to that act of unspeakable brutality against a harmless, little dog called Barker. The response was instantaneous. The Laika Institute was founded with the sole agenda of pursuing a programme of ruthless cleansing missions to avenge violations, past and present. Man... you should not have done that!

No time to spare now, he moves swiftly down the corridor past the battery of pods housing the navigator chickens, all charged for the next mission, all ready and waiting to be assigned to their Venge-Dog, all primed to point to the kill. Pressing on through three more doors, he reaches Recoop 48, in the bowels of the institute. Once inside, he blinks to adjust to the eerie half-light given off by the sea-blue walls. As always, he suffers a brief moment of nausea. The Handler insists it helps soothe them, placate them. And what the Handler says goes.

Without so much as a glance at the cages – he'd already decided which one he would take – Tupoc stumbles across the compound, almost tripping over the big, yellow, bendy tunnel in his haste. Stifling a curse, he hurries over to his bay, fires up his spool gun and grabs a length of wire. He has to work fast...

On returning to the foyer, he finds Uriq sat propped up against the far wall, a used fire extinguisher by his side. A trickle of foam dribbles from the corner of his mouth. Ankl is lying on his back on top of the counter, staring wide-eyed at the ceiling. Tupoc had rehearsed the line he was going to spin to them, but there is no need. The luludust is seriously good kadonka.

'*I got the munchies*,' drools Uriq.

'*Me too. You know what I'm gonna do when I get home?*'

'*What?*'

'*I'm gonna rip off Juanita's clothes and smear Marmite all over her naked body, and then lick it all off.*'

Uriq pauses to think. '*You're gonna need about eight tubs.*'

As casually as he can, Tupoc makes his exit. '*Goodnight, guys*,' he waves.

'*Yubba-dubba-doo.*'

'*Anchovies!*'

***

Freaked by the ever-increasing frequency of pings echoing down the corridor, she has long since given up trying to piece together a monologue. It just won't work. The whole point is the dialogue between the two puppets. The original script had been perfect. Word perfect.

Instead, she spends her time staring at the wall, playing over in her mind what might have been. Of course, she hadn't told Xilox about the two trillion zecs she was going to hold back for herself – he'd be happy enough with his share. Of course, she hadn't told Tupoc about the two trillion zecs she was going to hold back for herself. It was going to be a surprise. He was coming with her.

They'd buy a beat-up camper truck and head out to the

Rim for a bit of desert dirty. Then over the tundra to the Cap, where they'd sit in hot springs, fish for halibiff through holes in the ice, smoke elk leaf and chew tonka moss together. It would have been wonderful, so wonderful...

Staccato knocks at the dressing room door. 'Calling Emily Weintraub! Calling Emily Weintraub!'

With a heavy sigh, she picks up Dino and drags her feet over to the door. She opens it, only to be bundled back into the room by a breathless Tupoc.

'*You came back!*' she breathes.

'*I said I would,*' he nods. He undoes his coat to reveal a sight which makes her tonsils wibble – a perfect, sap-size puppet.

'*He looks so... real,*' she purrs.

'*He does,*' he coughs.

'*But what? How...?*'

'*Don't ask. Quick, let me show you how he works. I've attached two wires, here... to open and close his mouth and here... to make his head swivel. Here, you try.*'

As if she were being handed a newborn for the first time, she takes him to her. He not only looks real, he *feels* real. He is beautiful...

With her free arm, she pulls Tupoc tight to her and puffs in his ear. '*Dog only knows what I'd be without you.*'

He licks the tip of her nose. '*Go kill 'em, Tank!*'

All she can see is an array of bright amber slits of pupil life shining up at her from the wall of darkness. She steps out onto the apron. A couple of tails thump the floor, as if to say get on with it, it's been a long evening. Inhale, hold for five seks, exhale. Get that heart rate down to seventeen. Breathe in...

hold… breathe out.

Ook, the stage is much larger than it looked from down there. Ook, it's so bright up here. Ook, it's so black out there. The elderly couple right in front of her had clearly been traumatised by the tightrope fellatio, but a sneaky sideways glance at the scoreboard tells her that the acrobatic sex is leading, with a score of… she gulps… 756!

She climbs onto the stool, balances Dino on one knee and new Enzo on the other, parts her lips, fixes the smile, inhales through the nostrils and…

Ping! Ping! Ping, ping, ping, ping, ping, ping, ping… ping!

Red pings. And she hasn't even started yet! From the corner of her right eye, she catches a movement which betrays the culprit. Front row. Single occupant. Thick-rimmed glasses. Stupid grin on his face. Clipboard Diq!

Now everything falls into place: him keeping his distance; the funny smile across the factory floor; her stolen puppet. She would have him, and it would be sweet, without mercy. But right now, she has to deal with the number of pings stacking up on the board behind her. His ten have triggered an alarming run on the red. She parts her lips, fixes the smile, inhales deeply through the nostrils, opens Dino's jaws and…

"Good evening, Citizens of Cinnabar!"

The Crumple Zone folds in on itself, as all the air is sucked out. An electric frenzy zips across the cavern:

'*Sapspeak!*'

'*Diktat 7!*'

'*Sacrilege!*'

'***I'm here!***'

'*Salt mines!*'

'*Panic!*'

'I'm here!'

'Faaark!'

'Escape!'

First to rise, from the table nearest the door, is a skinny male.

'Sit down, Axl,' comes the command from his wife, cutting through the panic static like a hot knife through butter. *'It's a fuckn puppet! Now go get me another pitcher of tequila.'* She smacks her green button.

The loud green ping puts a handbrake on all thought of flight. *'She's right. It's only a dummy.'*

'I wasn't scared. The girl isn't speaking sap. I'm not speaking sap. Nobody's speaking sap. And isn't that The Tank?'

"Hi everyone, my name's Dino. We have with us tonight a guest from Planet Earth. Look at him, a real sap."

Ping, ping, ping, ping...

"Hope you don't mind me calling you a sap, sir. Much easier than *Homo sapiens.* And, some would say, more accurate."

Tails thump as buttons are pressed,

"But, hey, why should I apologise? I have to say, I can get quite upset when I hear saps taking my name in vain."

Enzo turns to Dino to speak for the first time. "I don't understand. How do you mean?"

"Well, when you call someone a dinosaur, what do you mean?"

"I mean... someone who can't cope with – or refuses to cope with – a changing environment."

"Well, I don't know about you, audience, but I call that ever so slightly fuckn cheeky."

Ping, ping, ping...

'Oh, she is sooo zoic!'

"Can you tell me, Enzo, how long the dinosaurs were on that rock which you now inhabit?"

"Er..."

"Let me tell you. It was 165 million Earth years, give or take. And how long has your breed been there?"

"Er..."

"Let me tell you. For 6.5 million of your years, tops. And you won't see 7, that's for sure."

Tails thump. Buttons ping.

"I beg to differ. We stand as the most intelligent species ever to have lived on Earth. And you, the dinosaur, are extinct."

"Really? And really?"

"Of course. You were wiped out when a meteor struck Earth and caused a nuclear winter. Everyone knows that."

"Meteor?"

"Yes. Left a massive crater, somewhere in Mexico."

"Chicxulub crater, Yucatán Peninsula?"

"Yes, that's the one!"

"Hate to burst your bubble, sap..." *Giggle, giggle, giggle, ping, ping, ping...* "but that was no meteor. That was the blast-off crater left by our mother ship, *Red Rover 1*."

"But, but, wasn't the dinosaur species almost totally wiped out?"

"Sad but true. Sacrifices had to be made. They died to save us all."

"No, that's nonsense! You're just making this up. I seem to recall that meteor deposits were found in fossil digs."

"Rocket exhaust debris. Sure, sap palaeontologists do the best they can, but they over-rely on primitive technology, like the rest of your kind."

"What are you talking about?"

"Saps put all their energy into the wrong kind of technologies that will end up destroying their world. I would liken your position to that of a bubble floating down a river of raw sewage towards a spiny cactus..." *Ping, ping, ping, ping, ping...* "if only you'd stuck to parchment and quill, you wouldn't be on a one-way street to robokrieg."

Enzo shakes his head.

"You've literally lost touch with your earth. You wear shoes, for dog's sake! Look, you're even wearing a pair now!"

"Ha ha, all very funny. The wise words of Dino the doll. You seem to forget, you're not a real dinosaur – you're a puppet."

Dino shakes his head. "So, you really think I am extinct, do you?"

Enzo nods.

"Well, I think you should just turn round and take a look at whose knee you're sitting on. Why do you think her stage name is **VeeVee**, the velociraptor ventriloquist?"

The crowd erupts. The ping counter hits 800. She's won!

***

The fire escape door beside the stage bursts in with a crash. That can mean only one thing – it's a raid!

'*Freeze!*' snarls the dog squad kommandant as the lights go up.

Emily notices that the chair once occupied by Clipboard Diq is empty. He's grassed them, the little snakefuck!

Behind the bar, Stog holds his head in his hands. '*Why do*

they always do this? They know they can just walk through the wall. Why do they have to be so dramatic?'

There are seven of them, of course. Six swiftly move to take up position around the locale to block off all escape routes, while the kommandant pads up onto the stage, Havana in mouth, the fox red lustre of its perfectly groomed coat gleaming in the spotlights.

'I have received intelligence that sapspeak has been expressed here. Diktat 7 has been breached. Who is the perpetrator?'

Silence.

'If you are so proud of this discredited tongue, use it now to confess your sins.'

Silence.

'And before you even think about it, I don't have time for any of that "I am Spartacus" crap. My patience is as wafer-thin as the pathetic excuses now formulating in your minds. Speak now!' it growls.

Silence.

'Then so be it! Your stillness serves as an admission of guilt. You shall share collective responsibility for what has passed here. You shall pay for your loyalty to sapspeak. You shall each serve seventy long moons in the Laxdoop mines.'

Emily Weintraub – alias The Tank – opens her mouth to speak. To her horror, the sap puppet spasms into life, turns his head towards her, blinks twice, hops off her knee and totters to the front of the stage. There, he dances a little jig and sings:

> *Auntie Mary*
> *Had a canary*
> *Up the leg of her drawers.*

When she farted,
It departed,
To a round of applause.

Auntie Mary
Had a canary
Up the leg of her drawers.
When she farted,
It departed
To a round of applause.

The End...

Printed in Great Britain
by Amazon

44441371R00081